# THE LOST PROPHECY

MAANAT BHADANI

Copyright © Maanat Bhadani
All Rights Reserved.

This book has been published with all efforts taken to make the material error-free after the consent of the author. However, the author and the publisher do not assume and hereby disclaim any liability to any party for any loss, damage, or disruption caused by errors or omissions, whether such errors or omissions result from negligence, accident, or any other cause.

While every effort has been made to avoid any mistake or omission, this publication is being sold on the condition and understanding that neither the author nor the publishers or printers would be liable in any manner to any person by reason of any mistake or omission in this publication or for any action taken or omitted to be taken or advice rendered or accepted on the basis of this work. For any defect in printing or binding the publishers will be liable only to replace the defective copy by another copy of this work then available.

Dedicated to my parents, mentors and SMVS

# Contents

# CHAPTER ONE

# THE LOST PROPHECY

In small opening through the hallway, almost invisible to the outside world, there lied a door which led to a room, about which no one knew. It went un-noticed by other students but James would always speculate about it; always caught his green alluring eyes. "Hey buddy!" came a voice from somewhere and abruptly prompted George from nowhere leaving James perplexed for a minute. "Hey George!" replied James in a total confused manner. "What's up with you?"

"Nothing, just pondering about a thing or two."

"Why would you lie James; you know that you are despicable at lying" shouted out Romilda.

"What do you mean Romilda?" "I saw you gawk at that room like an imbecile boy"

"No, no, no! it is just getting up my nerve."

"I don't have the faintest clue that why does that room in the whole school always catch up my eyes"

"Yes but it is restricted for students for a reason which school doesn't want us to know"

"Yes I know I really try holding back and not talking about it." said James seeming to be confused.

James could not have an invigorating sleep since days because of it. Slept on the bed, he lay like a dead body contemplating about the mysterious and hideous restricted room in his school. He was hell-bent to set his foot into that room and perceive its contents. Out of the blue moon, he suddenly thought of a plan to help his anxiety. He went up to Romilda and George directly in his break and dictated them about his plans. "James! How could you even think about it" whispered Romilda enraged and trying to be soft at the same time which was getting onerous. George was simply standing there awestruck. "You ok George??" George waking to his senses said out some words which were exceedingly unclear. "I would stop you right there George and I know what you want to express" "James, this is totally absurd and I would love to stop you right there" said Romilda "Yes, James, I know that it is worrying you but you need to control yourself and restrict yourself from doing what you are talking about" said George sounding concerned.

"Guys, I know that this is a dull-witted idea" "You think??, Of course it is!" said Romilda "Try to understand; I will get an anxiety attack" "Sleeping at night is proving to be a difficult task for me nowadays because I cannot keep my mind off that room" "I have a master key; let's go in and just have a quick look" James took some time but in some time, he managed to convince them to come with him "From where did you manage to obtain this key though??" questioned Romilda "Will explain it later; let's jump right in" "And come right out" added in Romilda. James was already quite displeased by Romilda, showing no support for him. James unlocked the lock and gradually moved in. The creeping of the door raised the intense pool of fear deep within Romilda and George. James' face was turning pale as he steadily opened the door. The room wore a black mask and not a thing was visible. However, the triplet walked in with courage in search of a source of light or a small torch. They, in a hurry searched for one. "Ouch!" squeaked George "What happened George?" `asked James and Romilda; their senses were triggered and George's squeak added to the build-up of intense fear in their minds. "Nothing, something fell on my head" George bent down to feel something metallic right by his feet. Picking it up, he started scrambling the surface of the object trying to figure out what it was. Suddenly a bright flash came out of the same and the room was filled with a dull yellow light. He found a switch for the lights in the room. Turning the switch on soaked in the darkness and the dullness of the room; so, did their fear. They breathed a sigh of relief but on seeing the dusty and untidy room they were surprised, strongly believing that whatever they performed till now was nothing but a waste of time. James' opinion differed strongly from theirs and was going through all the contents in the room closely as if he were a detective. The room emerged like a left-out storage shed from an old house in a school. "There is nothing here James that is to be kept so preciously!" said Romilda frustrated. "Why do you think that they would make this particular room restricted even for the senior most students; there has to be a reason behind it!" replied James in a stressful tone searching for anything unique and distinct object. "James, there is nothing here worth staying for except for dirt and all these rusty objects which we are clearly not interested in" said Romilda "We haven't even searched properly yet and I have a robust feeling that there is something suspicious here which is concealed extremely thoughtfully from a human eye." "Of course, you won't find it until you search deliberately for it" "I reckon we are the one among the many imprudent people alive on who don't have an idea about what are they even searching for." said George directing the taunt towards James indirectly. James ignored his words and kept working his way through all the things in the room analysing each extremely carefully and cautiously making sure that he is not making a lot of noise. "Hey, can you hear the footsteps??" cried out Romilda. "YES!!!!, I thing that someone has suspected our presence in this room," said George. "Hurry up! Hide anywhere you can and switch off the light" They struggled searching for an appropriate place to conceal themselves. Romilda switched off the light being the nearest to the switch board. They all hid themselves in the dark hoping that the person doesn't spot them behind a cupboard. As the noise of the footsteps increased and the person seemed to be approaching closer and closer to them, their heartbeats increased exponentially. The creaking door was opened by the person. All three of them had hid themselves in one dark corner of the room behind a sloppy cupboard standing with the support of the wall. They had found some place behind the cupboard. The lights were switched on. The person was a guard. He started interrogating the place. He was coming close by and the fear in their heart rose intensely. "Who is there!!" screamed the guard proceeding to come nearer to their hiding spot "Now only god can save us; we are screwed" whispered George "Shhh!!!" replied Romilda trying to stay silent and not let the guard suspect their presence in shabby enclosed room. Suddenly a thundering shrill came from outside. The guard ran outside the room. He switched the lights off and locked the creepy door. "That was so close." said James taking a sigh of relief. "This is all your fault James!!; we were so close to getting caught red handed lingering around this spooky place" said Romilda pushing herself out of the compact space behind the cupboard. "That was the world's most uncomfortable place I have ever hid in! I had to hold my breath for the time I was in there because you both were squishing me out like a sponge ball" complained George. "I am sorry guys but let's not argue now." said James accepting his mistake. "Ouch! My head" squeaked James's bumping into something

George speedily switched on the light so that the happenings in the room start turning out clearer for all three of them. "Thanks a lot George," said Romilda. "My pleasure" replied George. "Are you fine James" asked George "Yeah! I am totally fine; just randomly bumped into this brick sticking out of the wall; couldn't see this because of the dark" said James "That is so uncanny; when we were getting in here, there was no such brick like this and all of a sudden it appeared out of nowhere" said George "Anyways, let's get out of this place or else we will be screwed." whispered Romilda. "Wait!" interrupted James before Romilda could go on further and convince them to get out of that room. "Are you sure George that this brick wasn't sticking out when we were squeezing in here." Interrogated James "Yes, I am extremely sure because my head actually was touching this part of the wall when we hid here." "Ohh! Now this is falling into place." "What happened James??" asked Romilda sounding extremely perplexed. "Just watch here" replied James. James started gently sliding his hand over the bricks and then started pushing in some bricks. One brick made a snapping sound and there was rumbling sound in the other far end corner of the room. It started opening a hidden compartment. "Wooahhh!" screamed George looking with awe and perplexity at the same time towards the gently sliding walls divulging its secrets which were being discussed since all three of them joined the school. A splash of anticipation and happiness evoked inside his body giving him goosebumps all over.

Gradually descending the stairs, all three of them were surprised on seeing the charm of the room filled with variant shades of light entering the room as if it were passing through a humongous prism and meeting their eyes. "Holy moly!" squeaked George "Who could have even guessed the existence of such a ravishing and eye pleasing place beneath an old, rusty and shabby room." "No one!" replied Romilda filled to brim with awe and disbelief. "I had told you guys that there is something in this room or else why would it be restricted," said James. "I did not understand that why would they keep this room restricted if there is nothing that is hazardous or anything that should be kept away from a person's eye." said George. "Yes, I am also quite a bit confused." added in Romilda. "At this point everything is just bouncing off my head too." Said James. "Anyways let's just look at the alluring chamber we have in front of our eyes; not sure whether we will be able to witness something such attractive again or not" "True!" said Romilda. They started strolling around the chamber and feeling the soft mushy flowers on their hand to give themselves a tinge of relaxation after the stressful events that just took place. They all were silent for an awkwardly long time pondering here and there wondering about the location of the chamber and even its existence which wasn't introduced to them by the school. The charm of the room gradually took over the robust confusion and anxiety in their heads. Suddenly James saw a peculiar box with a lot of variant designs carved out on it camouflaged between two shelves, seemed as if someone was trying to hide it. There were some letters carved out on it but James was unable to read given it was in a different language which he had never come across. Its surface was covered in moisture and algae had formed all over it because of it. It seemed ancient by its looks.

"James' curiosity level rose higher and higher by constantly focusing his eyes on the box. There was no visible latch nor a keyhole to open the box up. This further contributed in helping anxiety and curiosity inhabiting his mind. "Hey Romilda and George; come here, I found something that might interest you both" called out James. "What is that in your hand?" asked Romilda "I also don't have an idea about this." answered James "It just looked interesting so I picked it out" "Let me have a look at it" said George taking away the box from James' hand. "How do you open it up?" "If I had an idea, I would have opened it up minutes ago" replied James

"Let me have a look George," said Romilda. Romilda observed the box's details extremely carefully noting every single fragment of artwork sculpted on it. "Do you know that in which language is this text on this box written in?" Romilda and George started mulling over and recalling all the past history lessons in the past. They pondered over the topic for a long time but they ended up with no result. "So, what do we do now?" asked George. "We forget about this box and mend our ways" replied Romilda "What do you mean by mend our ways" "James, we have been here since a long time which we were not meant to." "Don't you realise that we are still breaking the school rules staying in here; you told me that we will get out soon but it has been hours since we came in here" "Chill out Romilda; catch some breath first" "And by the way didn't you realise this when we came in this underneath hidden chamber" replied James "I got distracted by these captivating objects which I have never seen any day before in my 16-year life!" "Exactly! We have never seen these objects ever before in our lives and God knows when we will be able to witness a library of such attractive objects again." "Guys! Stop arguing, you are getting a bit loud and there are still chances that a person might be able to hear specks of our conversation by just standing closer to the door." Interrupted George leaving a long silence in the room. Suddenly, a high pitched and tumultuous sound reached out towards them out of nowhere. Confusion took over their minds within a second. "Guys! This sound is coming from the box we were fiddling around with" shrieked George. Before someone could grab the box, the sound gradually faded out leaving a robust impact in their ears. "My ears are still ringing from that sound" cried Romilda in a painful tone. James grabbed the box and noticed a small crack. There was not only, but multiple cracks which started forming on this box." "Look carefully at the crack guys, they are forming a repeated pattern. They gazed at the box bewildered and awestruck at the same time trying to process the events taking place in front of their eyes. "At this point I don't believe my eyes anymore" George "I totally agree with you George" supported Romilda.

"Shall we leave this place and save our skin?" said George out of fear "Wait a moment! It is opening up" replied James. The box opened up gradually casting out a bright light which their eyes could not handle. Reflecting every single object in the room the light created an array of rays. There lied a prophecy in the box made out of pure glass, and it was so clean as if it was never ever touched by anyone since it was created. James took out the prophecy out of the box admiring the work of crafts work done on it. Encrypted there were some other weird numbers on them which was not their cup of tea to understand. "Not this weird language again!" cried Romilda. "This is probably an extremely ancient thing; if I am right" "I cannot agree more!" replied Romilda. James gently held the object in his hands as the prophecy seemed fragile. Suddenly all the colours of the light started showing one by one in the globe; seeming like a transition of blank to a radiant prophecy. All three of them were still surprised by the fact that they were still not caught by anyone. But they could not care less about the same.

"This is the strangest thing that has ever happened to me" said James in a low tone. "Forget about that; but what are we waiting for." "Let's get out of here or else we will be caught soon." "I don't anticipate that we are going to leave any time soon" said Romilda "And what make you think that? "Asked George filled up with bewilderment. "Look at James, and it will answer your question" replied Romilda "Ahhh! Got it" "You got some taunts aimed towards me today" replied James sounding frustrated. "I realize that we have spent way too much time lingering around here but let's just try to understand this prophecy given that we have already picked it up." "You picked it up!" "And we must not further waste time wandering around here or else we will be screwed" James was no longer hearing a thing. He was extremely busy examining the prophecy still giving out bright light. Romilda was exasperated by James and she could not control her actions. She became more and more furious every second. She snatched the prophecy from James' hands and smashed it on the ground shattering it into a million pieces. "What did you do Romilda!!" shrieked James enraged by Romilda's actions. James stepped forward to gather pieces of the prophecy but was stopped by George. "James, chill! it is just a prophecy; it doesn't provide any reason for you to hurt yourself and pickup these shattered pieces." Said George trying to control James' sentiments. "I strongly advice you both that forget about all the events that have taken place in the past hours and let's get out of here before we get caught"

"Yes let's go; Romilda has left us no reason to stay here any longer" taunted James "Finally!!, you are listening to someone" said Romilda with a sigh of relief. James was extremely furious and this triggered his anger even further. "Stop it, Romilda!" intervened George.

They had begun ascending the stairs but immediately the doorway which allowed them in closed.

"I reckon that the door would have slid in on its own as it was really heavy and we didn't put it straight up." Said James "Let's try opening it up then" added in George James and George sweated themselves out but the door didn't open up at all. In fact, it didn't even move an inch from its position. "What do we do now?" asked Romilda in a tone of panic and confusion. "We are trapped here," said James. "I realise that but what do we do then?" asked Romilda.

"I don't' know, I haven't even been in such a situation ever in my life before." "Well now we are in one; think about this." "We can't just keep on endeavouring and keep hoping to open this door up." "We need a solid plan or some kind of tool," said Romilda. "There are many things here; we can use them to help us," said George. "Great idea!" They rushed towards different aisles and started hurriedly searching for an object that can perform a heavy-duty task. Swiftly running from one corner of the room, they could not find any object that would be useful for them. The room was filled up with all sorts of fragile objects which was of total no use for them. A scent started spreading throughout the room and quickly approached James', Romilda's and George's nose.

"What is this appalling smell!!" shouted out George. "Keep it low George". "We can still be heard."

"But what is this smell; it is killing me!" "I don't have any idea" whispered James

"I reckon we must forget about the smell and keep searching for something solid," said Romilda.

"I agree but this smell is up my nose and it is extremely horrible." Whispered George painfully

"Stop cribbing George; I can also smell it but you need to bear with the circumstances for a minute to get out of this situation." James started looking for an object while Romilda was preaching George about 'bearing the pain'. He saw a faint light too from somewhere. When he followed the light; the smell just got stronger. When he reached the roots of the smell, he noticed the shattered prophecy lying there giving out a sea green light and it was the source of the smell. He quickly dashed towards Romilda and George filled with consternation unknown of anything.

"Guys!! This smell is coming from the shattered pieces of the prophecy" screamed James full of perplexity and anxiety

"What are you talking about!!" screamed back George "How can that thing practically generate a smell so robust that after it is shattered." "I would agree with George" said Romilda "If you don't believe me go have a look!" shouted James frowning at the fact that he was not believed upon. "Yeah, let's go and have a quick look." Said George Romilda and George dashed towards the place where they witnessed the shattering of the prophecy into a million pieces. George and Romilda were shocked upon reaching the place where the prophecy lay shattered. "James, you were right!" squeaked Romilda

"I knew that I was right" said James "Sarcasm at its peak James." Added in George

"Let's leave this spot at the moment or else the consequences can be severe!" said Romilda

Out of the blue moon, a light started flashing out of the prophecy's shattered pieces which was gradually sucking in some of the things in the room. Fear started tingling through their mind and they were not able to process the events happening around them.

"What are we waiting for; let's run-away" shrieked George out of sheer fear.

They began to run in the opposite direction of the current that was generated by the mysterious prophecy but their efforts went into vain as the current grew stronger every minute acting like a black hole.

They grabbed a pipe attached to a wall but the pipe gave up its life and all three of them went into the prophecy.

They felt nauseous as they went into the everlasting loophole of the prophecy.

"Ouch! My head hurts a lot" said James

"Mine too!" added in George having no clue of what just happened in the past minutes of his life

"Where are we?" asked Romilda filled up with a bust of emotions.

As the three of them looked around, they found several trees and bushes. Their minds stormed with one question again and again.

"We are stranded in a forest by the looks of our surroundings!" squeaked James

"Yes, and this is all because of you and your stupid room." Said Romilda

"Don't put the blame on me; If you would have had a speck of patience and not snatched the prophecy from my hand, this all would have not happened." Countered James

"And who wanted to have a LOOK in the room which was RESTRICTED!" "If you would have some control over yourself and acted like a sane and a sensible person, we would not have to go in the room in the first place and be stranded in this terrifying place about which we don't have the slightest idea."

"Does not look terrifying by the looks of it though," said George

'That is because we do not know about it yet" replied Romilda in a loud tone.

"Cannot agree more with that too" said George" "Anyways, think about how will we get out of this forest" said George

"Yes, I agree with you George; and Romilda, I realise that us being here is all my fault but I do have the same frustration level as you so I got out of control and I am sorry for that." Apologised James in a sincere tone

"Yes, I apologise too; I also overreacted several times." Replied Romilda

"That is what I like!!" exclaimed George

Soon it started pouring and it was evening time. The light from the sun was blocked by the clouds leaving only darkness around them. The clouds were growling and roaring as it vigorously rained started raining. The clouds wrestled dropping sweat in form of thick blobs of raindrops which soon started hurting Romilda, James and George. The sky wore a black mask blocking every single speck of sunlight that was available to them making their situation nothing less than worse. In a matter of seconds, they were soaked, unable to find a place where they could spend the night. In a matter of seconds, the rain stopped and the frost replaced it.

Instead of mud and water, frost climbed up their bone making them feel colder than ever.

"I have never been in a worse condition than this; I am cold and soaked" Cried George

"If this is bugging you then, what would happen if we will not be able to even find a place to live out here."

"This is to inform you that you are not helping my mental health by saying this" Said George out of frustration

"Think this situation as another perspective; like you are just looking at another phase of life and you are just gaining experience out of this." Said James trying to cheer George up. "This phase seems like it will last forever." Added in Romilda slimily

"Romilda, what is the matter with you?" asked James

"Yes, you are being too negative!" whispered George weary from walking around for a long time.

"I don't know but my mind is revolving around all the bad things that have happened in the past couple of hours." "I am sorry and I will try my best to be a bit positive."

"Yes thanks a lot and let's find a shelter" said George

They ambled around the dark, thick and cold forest for a long time but there was no sign of food nor any shelter. The forest was damp, moist covered with mud housing a lot of insects which made them feel more miserable as time passed by.

"Guys let's give ourselves a bit of rest or else we will pass out soon." Said James "I cannot agree more." Added in George "Let's sit beneath that tree on that huge rock."

Meanwhile they tried to make themselves comfortable on the hard rock which was hurting their bottoms, James found a bush full of cranberries. He plucked most of them and handed them to George and Romilda and kept some for himself.

"Guys have some cranberries; these might help in replenishing some energy."

They quickly stuffed their mouths with a handful of them. A burst of flavour, sweetness and moisture ran through their mouth. "Umm these are the most palatable cranberries I have ever had in my entire life." Said George with a stuffed mouth expressing his gratification and contentment that the cranberries had given to him. "Slow down mate; you are stuffing your way too fast, you might choke."

They devoured on some cranberries filling up their stomachs and packed some for the rest of the way.

The only problem was that they didn't know where to go next and were again centralised in the zone of confusion.

"Those cranberries were juicy enough to delay my thirst for water but sooner or later we all might need water and we can't rely on these for a long time.; they will exhaust at one point." Said Romilda

"Yes, we will have to find a constant source of food and water to keep us going."

"How can we even find one; we have never been here and neither do we have a map nor do we have a person to assist us." Said George expressing his frustration.

"Yes we will have to reply strongly on our intelligence and search for a shelter or else we are done for good."
"After we find an appropriate place to house ourselves, we will have to find a way to get out of this place."

"Yes, let's keep penetrating through the place; if we are fortunate enough, we might find a dry cave around here."

They kept themselves going picking up some more fruits that they found on their way. Their pants were getting heavier and heavier from the excess moisture from the rain and fruits that they had to keep in their pockets as they did not have a backpack or anything to carry the fruits.

They walked until their eyes hit the naked sky which was soon clear of clouds and the stars were much more visible.

They could clearly see everything and spotted smoke coming from somewhere nearby them. It seemed like a huge fire had just broken out because the smoke was climbed up a great height.

"Do you think we should chase that fire??" asked James

"I don't have an idea; maybe we should actually, what if there be some people there who can assist us which we really require at this point."

"Yes, let's go there" added in Romilda

They ran with all the energy they had left in them towards them. However, the smoke wasn't too far so they reached their destination early.

On their arrival they could not see anything because the smoke didn't allow them to see through it.

"Hello; is someone there!!" shouted out James

They were only replied with the profound silence of the thick forest which was eventually broken by the noisy crickets that lay in the bushes.

"There was no point coming here." "We just wasted a bunch of energy just to experience cough created by the smoke." Cried George in a painful tone.

"No, our efforts didn't go in vain; notice that the sticks are collected and put in certain order to light up the fire."

Replied Romilda

"I know where you are going; you mean that there is someone here in this dark, cold and scary place like us." Said James trying to put things together

"Exactly!!" said Romilda

"If we find this person; it will make our jobs way easier." Said George understanding everything gradually but steadily.

"Hey but it will probably be a bad idea to go searching right now as it is dark like coal and we might not be able to see many animals around us due to this." Said Romilda

"So what do we do now?" "George this is what I am pondering about too; wait for a moment."

They began to think about what do next, meanwhile James engaged himself in searching around the fireplacc to find any traces or a cave like structure where they could spend the rest of their safely. Comfort was not an option for them right now.

James felt cold breeze on his cheeks so he quit searching and went near the fireplace to catch some warmth for himself. While he was walking back to the fireplace, he could see a neatly stacked pile of leaves. He didn't bother to stay and have a quick look. Suddenly a relatively strong breeze swept past him destroying the mountain of leaves revealing a small opening.

"Romilda, George, come here right now." Called out James

Romilda and George were startled at first by James' loud and high-pitched voice. Romilda and George were astonished by what lay near the scrambled leaves.

"That is a cave!!" exclaimed George

"lord Jesus sent us help!" said Romilda sounding extremely holy at this point

They entered the cave through the opening which was just large enough for one person to go through it.

The cave was warm, colossal and dark from inside helping them attain warmth and comfort which they were craving since they had ended up in this mysterious cave.

It took them no time to make themselves comfortable and light up a fire from bonfire which was already burning a bit so that everything in the cave becomes much more visible to their naked, moist eyes and the fire helped themselves dry themselves up.

"Finally, I feel a bit comfortable but we need water and food too." "I can't go to sleep empty stomach and thirsty." Said George

"Here take these guys." Said James handing them a handful of cranberries to help themselves.

"These cranberries were flavoursome and appetizing at first when I tasted them but now my tongue is craving something else." Cribbed George

"George; do you realise that we are not eating these cranberries ourselves for luxury or taste; we are eating these to survive which is the most important thing right now for us." Said Romilda

"Romilda is right George; these cranberries can fill up your stomach and they are quite juicy so they can take care of the thirst too."

"I get it guys." Said George

The night had approached and they talked for a while about a thing or too and then were fast asleep on the dirty floor itself which they didn't care about as they were all worn-out and sapped.

The morning approached and the sun was high up in the sky.

They had no track of time and only knew that it was morning time.

The fire had set out but the sunshine was enough to give them enough warmth to still keep them comfortable.

Romilda opened her eyes up gradually which were directly hit by the bright sunshine. She eventually woke up and eventually ended up waking James and George from their deep sleep.

"Guys, it's morning; wake up!" said Romilda having enough loudness in her voice to wake both of them up at the same time

"Ahh, my back hurts a lot; feels like I slept on a stone." Said George

"I agree, my back is all stiff; I guess the floor was quite hard on our backs." Said James

"I felt like I had displaced one of the bones in my back bone when I woke up but then I stretched a bit and it was better." Said Romilda

"Let's go out and find the person who probably set off the bonfire yesterday." Said James.

"We will have to probably search the whole forest and then too there can be a good chance that we won't be able to find him or her; whoever the person is." Said Romilda

"I think we should go on a quest for a river too so that we can have a constant source of freshwater." Said George

"We can also find the person on the way."

"So, let's get moving and we can have some fruits on the way if we find some; the cranberries are completely exhausted."

They were as fresh as ever and were walking on a good pace. However, the dark, thick forest was full of puddles of dirty water and their legs were covered in mud by all the pools of mud they stepped in.

They were already quite shabby since the last night

They could not feel anything else but moist and tenacious mud on themselves which would not leave their skin without some certain amount of water which was not available to them.

Soon they were exhausted and they couldn't find any trace of water and also had no idea about the unknown person they were frantically searching for.

Their misery grew second by second as the sun was directly overhead sending a ray of light giving the robust sensation of heat making them even more thirsty.

"We are unable to find any water nor are we able to find the person we reckoned existed." Moaned George

"Mate we are in the same position as you are in but moaning is not the solution to the problem." Replied James

"We have to keep the hunt for a permanent source of water or else we will not take much time for us to die due to the intense thirst." Said Romilda

They had to eventually rest under a tree to catch their breaths from all the intense walking under the layer of heat created by the sun.

They found shade and food but nothing that could satisfy their intense thirst for water.

The levels of frustration enlarged themselves because of the intense thirst.

They tried to catch some quick sleep to avoid the thirst but the thirst had prohibited that too.

James found himself lying on the ground, almost falling unconscious though managing to keep his eyes open looking at the open blue sky.

James almost passed out, but because of the quite atmosphere he could hear the faintest sound of running water.

James picked himself up which was an extremely difficult task for him at this point.

His legs vibrated and he felt all weak.

He followed the sound in hope of finding the treasure he wanted desperately which was water.

His eyes were half closed but his ears were wide open following the sound of the water. As he walked further the sound of running water became clearer and clearer.

Unknown of the fact he chased the sound eventually finding himself in front of a huge wide and lively river full of fresh water.

His first instinct was to dump his head into the river chugging a whole bunch of water in his mouth. He could feel the cool sensation of water while swallowing it in his oesophagus.

He didn't bother to take his head out of the fast-flowing river until he was out of breath.

He quickly gathered himself and remembered about Romilda and George who were also extremely thirsty.

He dashed towards the place where they were. He found them on the ground looking sicker than ever.

He ran back to the river trying to bring back as much water as much he could in his hands sprinkling it over them

"Is that water" said George weakly

"Yes, it is; follow me and you will find a river full of fresh water"

They both picked themselves up which took a lot of effort and followed James at an extremely slow pace. As they approached the river, they had the same reaction as James.

They both chugged a whole lot of water too.

Soon they also got their heads out of the water to catch some breath.

"How do you feel guys" asked James in a concerned tone

"It felt like I almost had touched death but just escaped it because of you." Said Romilda who was silent since a long time. They couldn't stop themselves thanking him until James started talking about something which was extremely important.

"We will have to strategize to ensure we have better living conditions at this time." Said James trying to make a plan in his head.

"Yes, first we will have to find a cave nearby the river or mark the route using some special objects which symbolise the way." Said George

They didn't have any luggage which was a good thing for them so they didn't have a hard time shifting if they find a cave near the river.

"So do we search or are we going with the other option?" asked Romilda

"I think it will be sensible to search for a cave nearby as the cave we are hanging on to right now is quite far from here which might limit some of our water accessibility; the weather is extremely uncertain here." Replied James answering Romilda in one long sentence

"Yes, but is it a good idea to go on for a search right now because we are quite fatigued right now from all the thirst and lack of food." Said George

"The weather is quite good right now and the visibility is also quite good so it makes sense to search right now only; if we delay this anymore, we might not be able to find it later." Added in James

"What is we just rest in the cave we have right now and pick up some food on the way and then get out of the cave to search for another shelter when the weather is amiable towards us." Said Romilda after analysing about the situation presented in front them after some time.

"Sounds like a plan!" agreed George almost the next second

James also agreed in a minute or so and they began their journey back to their shelter.

They searched for some food here and they were successfully able to get some fruits which was their daily meal now.

Many a times they got bit by some miniscule mosquitoes which irritated their skins up to an extent that they had to scratch their skins all the time while going back to their cave.

They arrived near the shabbily arranged leaves; probably some flew away from there because of the strong winds.

The cave had arrived and they went inside, sitting near the ash from the bon fire that they had ignited. Some pieces of wood were still fresh and were enough to light up another fire so they were all set up for the night if the weather would change and become freezing cold again.

They fell fast asleep talking to each other gradually.

The wind was blowing and it did touch their skin but the cold could not break their deep sleep.

Thunderstorm took off and several dozens of leaves were plucked off from the trees.

Leaves had almost blocked their cave but a small opening wasn't covered.

They slept for a long time and directly woke up in the morning.

The sunlight struck James' face directly breaking his sleep and waking him up.

James woke everyone up.

"Guys, let's check the weather outside." Said James

They took their sleepy heads and carried them to the entrance of the cave which was partially blocked.

They used up a whole bunch of their energy in removing all the blockers like stones and leaves but many came out to be quite useful for them so they made a separate pile of them. There were a whole bunch of stones and leaves that were thrown away but twigs and some fruits were stored in the cave on a carpet of leaves which they made so that none of the fruits get dirty.

Sunlight ran through and it came at the moment when the entrance was freed up.

"A lot of work right in the morning is not my cup of tea." Said George exhausted from the heavy-duty task that they just had to do.

"I can agree with you on this." Added in Romilda

"Come on let's stop talking and move towards the river to find another cave; and now that we have a whole bunch of stuff, we will have to carry this all to the new cave we find or if we manage to find one." Said James

"Okay boss!" said George

Romilda chuckled on hearing this.

There was a momentarily silence after which they started proceeding out of the cave in to the heart of the forest towards the river.

The route to the river from their cave was indeed long. They were getting used to the animals, irritating plants and mosquitoes and were dealing with them pretty well. But in order of learning to deal with them their body had to be bruised multiple times till the point that they would become immune to all the things.

They route was long and the sun was not helping them at this point as it heated up their bodies making their heads heavier and smothered in sweat. They reached the river after a somewhat lengthy and tiring journey. They all were fatigued and immediately sat down under a humongous green tree which seemed larger in size and width. They lay down for a bit.

"Anyone up for a wash in the river??" asked George in a low tone

"We can't be naked here as there is Romilda here too." Said James

"What if we just wear the clothes and hop in."

"We will get our ONLY pair of clothes wet"

"I would like to stop you there and say that our clothes are already dirty and if we go into the river, they will be cleaner; and about the wet thing, they can dry up eventually." Said Romilda

"We have plenty of time here; we can do that" added in George.

"Then why not, let's hop in." agreed James

They hopped in the river but the flow of the river was unexpectedly faster than they thought and they had to apply some effort to stay against up or they would flow away somewhere in the river.

Initially, the river seemed bottomless as they struggled to feel the surface of the river basin from their legs but gradually, they managed to find a shallow end near the corner of the river.

The river was freezing cold and but the warmth from the sun was helping them. Putting their heads down in the river was a difficult task for them to do as it helped lose their sensitivity of their skin.

They could feel their body go frigid but it also brought in some freshness in them which they craved since a long time; since the time they arrived apparently.

They got out of the water feeling fresher than replenishing the sense of cleanliness around them in themselves. They lay on the warm ground to dry themselves up. Minutes passed by and they got relatively dryer.

"Guys get up now; we have to search for a cave too." said Romilda

"Lots of work on our hands right now."

Grass speckled on their skins giving out itchiness all over their bare skin

"The grass is itchier than a mosquito bite."

"Probably we should wash our legs and hands again." "It might help the itching."

They approached the river again and cautiously dipped their legs and hands ensuring there is no more moisture on their clothes as they were already feeling like they were carrying a lot of loads on their backs because of the soaked clothes.

A tree branch awkwardly jutted out of the tree from the top penetrating a bunch of leaves. It was awkwardly shaped and hideous because of its height.

A number of insects were moving smoothly towards the tree.

"How weird that such number of insects are moving smoothly towards this tree with an extra hand." Said Romilda

"How does it even matter to us; might be an insect party or something." "Let them do their work and lets us start our quest for a shelter or else we will again have to wait till tomorrow."

"Yes leave them and start moving." Said James.

They started walking in a random direction unknown of the routes in the forest.

The forest majestically stood in front of them in the last 2 days and they still had no clue of most of the routes they were following. They crumpled and scampered across bushes penetrating some of them; temporarily deforming them. Creaky sounds from the trees and broken twigs when stepped upon freaked them out constantly. The began to set as it sucked some of the darkness.

"Is it just me or you guys are also starving."

"I am definitely starving."

"Let's stop for a quick meal then." Said James

"Did anything edible catch your eye while we strolled along a whole bunch of the forest?" asked James

"No" replied both Romilda and George

"Neither did I find anything; shall we just continue searching around and if we find some food; we can stop for a quick break."

"Sounds like a plan."

They continued walking but unexpectedly sat down for a small break as their legs were hit with a splash of soreness and agony due to the constantly wandering around the forest.

It seemed as if they were caught tightly by bad luck in its fist.

"Why do we have to amble so much."

"I might have lost a couple of pounds just pondering around in this mystical forest just for searching around for stuff."

"We can't complain about anything; save energy by talking less and walking more"

They continued their quest for food for a long time but they had hard luck locating some. Some cranberries were awkwardly lying around which they had to consume.

They could feel their scarfs hurting and they almost felt like they muscles would give up and burst out any moment.

The pain was improbable for a normal person and they could feel it significantly more with every step they took.

"My leg might have internal bleeding or something if I go on for any longer." Cried George

"I can feel the pain more and more with every single second passing by." Said Romilda

"Why is this forest so harsh on us." Cried James

As James finished his sentence, they could hear a deafening, ear-piercing and sounds in some distance from them. The sound was terrifying and sounded as if trumpet was directly blown into one's ears.

James, Romilda and George didn't move nor did they speak anything for a minute or so. There was an awkward silence after the loud and ear destructive sound which they couldn't digest nor process in one go.

Soon they could visualize some sparkles in the sky which looked like a SOS. It reflected multiple colours in the sky and it was obvious to them at this point that someone was asking for help.

"Should we go there?" asked Romilda

"Of course we should; someone might require help." Replied James

"But what if there is some kind of hazard there which might harm us too."

"Don't act like a weakling at this point; if you don't want to come then don't, I am going there."

Saying this James sprinted towards the origin of the SOS. At least what he estimated it to be. The sprint consumed most of his leftover energy away and James was out of breath by the time he reached there. Romilda and George were following him but had fallen behind because of the swift pace that James caught on.

James could hear a person moaning "Help!" as he approached the place. He foraged for the person like he foraged for food and water. He brushed past a thick bush and the mystical person was covered from head to toe in blood. He also looked aged from his wrinkles on the face and white hair. Besides him lay a small cannon like structure which he might have used to send out an SOS in the sky. He approached the person briskly

"How may I help you sir?" asked James in bewilderment as he didn't know about how to fix the person.

The person was making an effort to speak but was unable to due to the deep wounds that lay on his skin.

"Fetch me that bag." Said whispered the person in pain pointing towards a bag that lay silently in beneath the shade of a tree. James swiftly ran towards the bag and brought it to his possession.

"Do you want something from this bag which can help you sir?" asked James

"Hand me over the green vile from the last chain!"

James looked frantically for the same in the bag. In matter of seconds James had already found and opened up the vile.

He handed the vile over to the old man. The vile which was covered or marked with a large number of small spots or patches of colour with moisture reflecting back some colours of light spectrum into James' eyes. The old man carefully let two drops of the liquid pass by the filter of the vile into his mouth gradually. As he swallowed the drops, he lifted himself to let his back support against the tree more.

Romilda and George had already arrived but James could not sense their presence as he devote himself to the old man.

In a matter of seconds, blood started clearing off his body and it seemed as if he was healing himself.

The blood ran back into the possible minute pores of the human body, seeming like the veins are sucking the blood back into the seemingly aged body of the man.

"Woah, how is this happening?" asked George in awe

"Maybe he is a wizard or maybe a REAL magician." Replied Romilda

"Shush!! Let the person gain all his senses back and recover completely; then we will interview him peacefully." Said James

James caught a glance at him and he seemed much better

"Are you fine now?" asked James's sounding concerned about his health.

"There is progress; and thanks a lot for saving my life"

"If you wouldn't have come; I would have felt my graveyard in a matter of seconds."

"My pleasure sir"

"Do you want anything else or anything I can help you with." Asked James

"No son, you have helped me enough; I better get back to my village before it gets dark and you also go to your home."

"Night is certainly not the best time to linger around this thick forest." Said the old man.

"Hi sir my name is Romilda, this is James and this is George." Said Romilda introducing everyone to the old man

"May we know you good name sir?" asked Romilda

"My name is Andrew Bozila; I originate from a village named Meraki." Replied the old man

"How did you get yourself into this type of situation?" asked Romilda

"This forest is covered with various danger which you are probably unaware of; I stubbed my leg through a poisonous cactus plant."

"These are the most dangerous plants and probably the hazard you should stay away from."

"Actually we are not from here."

"This is a totally new place to us and we landed up here mysteriously."

"Long story short, we came here through an inexplicable prophecy."

"You are not the first one here to come here in this manner; I have seen people come in here every year and staying here for the rest of their lives." Said Andrew in a serous though weak tone

"You are frightening me at this point.; won't we be able to go to our home ever again." Said George

"You can but it is you should rather choose not to." Replied Andrew

"And before you go on and ask me anymore questions; let us go in a nearby cave I know so that we will have a cover from probable rain."

"Ok, let's move right now." Said James

Andrew took the lead and lead them to a nearby cave

It was starting to get dark now and the chameleon like atmosphere also was gradually turning cold now.

"We have reached the cave." Said Andrew

James, Romilda and George were bewildered as they could not visually see any sort of opening to a cave or even like a possible cave like structure.

"Where is the cave??" asked James

"Ahh, it is visually hidden so that animals cannot just creep into and feast on us while we are fast asleep."

"Smart move." Said George

Andrew removed the bushes and leaves from a stone which was covering the cave. A colossal rock showed up in front of their eyes. Gently stroking the rock, he pressed his hands into some specific spots.

Gradually a rumbling sound made way to their ears. The cave was passing on in front of their eyes slowly.

They glanced at the cave and as it opened, they brainstormed a million unanswered questions in their minds for Andrew.

They entered the cave with an ocean of confusion and doubt in their heads followed by Andrew.

"I have never been more confused in my entire life; Andrew I have a lot of questions for you and I am sure that Romilda and James would also have them too."

"Yes, I agree; my mind is overloaded with a crowd of questions." Said James

"I already knew that; just be a bit patient, we will have to prioritize some tasks first."

"And I still haven't recovered fully."

"First, we will have to light a fire and then have a nice meal."

After saying this they divided the tasks of finding wood for fire and cleaning up the old and rusty cave.

James went out seeking some hidden dry wood which they could possibly use to cook some food.

Meanwhile, Andrew already has some raw food which was required to be cooked properly before it could be consumed by any of them.

Romilda was helping George clean the cave so that they could make themselves even more comfortable.

They all were done with their work in a couple of minutes and soon they found themselves near the bonfire waiting eagerly for it to be light up so that they can escape from the wrath of the coolness of the atmosphere.

"How do we light up the fire; do you have any idea about this Andrew?"

"Hand me over my bag from that corner." Said Andrew contemplating about the contents of his bag

He dug his hand into the bag pulling out a thin vile of a type of liquid about which Romilda, James and George were unaware about.

He gave the vile a robust shake and carefully allowed a singular drop of orange, lustrous drop of it into the wood which was lying in front of them.

As the drop of the spectacular liquid touched the surface of the dry wood, it gave out a small splint in at start and gradually a marvellous fire was dancing in front of their eyes.

"I am quite fond of that bag that you carry around; does It universally have every single type of magical potion?" asked James

"No, it doesn't have every single kind of potion of course, but it has most of the potions which will help you survive; and you might have actually seen this by now."

"Yes, we already have examples of two situations." Said Romilda

"Does everyone own one of these in your village?" asked George out of curiosity

"No, not everyone can get their hands on these types of bags."

"These are specially handed over to the people in the village council." Said Andrew

"Now let's keep the rest of the talking for later and have our dinner now; I am starving." Said Andrew before anyone else could go on and ask another question.

They let the warmth of the bonfire to sink deep into their skins to comfort their hearts and soon started cooking fish on their natural stove.

As the fish started cooking, the odour of the cooked fish started spreading throughout the cave; James, Romilda and George let the robust odour which they hadn't felt in a long-time travel through their nostrils in two or three long breaths.

"The fish smells so good" said George

"I feel like taking the fish off the fire and feasting it on right now." Said James controlling his emotions.

"Have patience!!"

"You will have the chance to have this fish and equal amounts will be served to all as there is a limited number of them." Said Andrew

"Ok"

Andrew soon carefully took the fish sticks off the bonfire serving the fish equally to every single one of them in front of banana leaves which served as plates here.

"I have never had food on leaves ever before; seems like it is going to be quite a lot of fun."

"Back in Meraki, we have the tradition of eating food on banana leaves whenever there is an occasion."

As they talked Romilda and James were busy devouring on the delectable fish that lay in front of them.

Hunger took over the moment and George also started feasting upon the delicacy.

Soon their enduring hunger had taken a sleep and they could feel the effects of the same in their body.

"Having a proper meal feels satisfying."

"Proper nutrition is the key" said James

Romilda chuckled on the topic but remained silent for some time allowing the heavy meal to digest.

"Now let's go to sleep; you people need rest" said Andrew

"Even you will need rest" said Romilda

They dozed off in a matter of seconds and the warmth kept nurturing their comfort.

The sleeping conditions were relatively better as they managed to just get enough banana leaves to at least make a mat for every single person.

As the night in the forest passed by, the temperature fell down drastically stripping the warmth off them.

The cave was concealed and packed making it sound proof and filtering the cold out, which helped them considerably to continue sleeping.

As morning approached their doorstep, they managed to get their eyes open and freshen themselves up.

James and George could still feel a bit lethargic from the long sleep that they had just gotten up from.

Romilda was already off to the river to have a bath.

James, George and Andrew followed after some time and escaping from the wrath of laziness.

The river was the same as the last time they had seen it, jaunty, fast-flowing and frisky spirited with the gift of water.

The second thing that was visible to them after the ravishing river was Romilda shaking her head vigorously trying to dry off her hair. Humour took dominated the moment and James and George started laughing off loudly immediately.

Romilda was startled and screamed out "Who is it!!"

"Your friends are laughing at you because you were drying off your hair in a somewhat unusual manner." Said Andrew

James and George could not stop their burst of laughter so Andrew had to answer for them.

Romilda was embarrassed and blurted out the first excuse she could have possibly thought of.

"I wasn't drying my hair; something was stuck in my head so I was trying to get it off me."

"Let me take a wild guess; insanity was stuck in your head right." Said James mocking Romilda

On hearing this Andrew also started chuckling unable to hold his emotions.

"There could have been a million excuses you could have thought off but this I surely the lamest and the most hilarious you could have picked out." Said George

"Oh come on, now stop this!!" said Andrew trying to save Romilda from further embarrassment by the boys

James and George stopped their laughter soon but this event was saved as a photographic memory in their heads.

"Go and have a bath; the water is quite warm because of the Sun." said Romilda trying to change the topic.

"Sure dancing lady" said James as they proceeded towards the river.

They stripped off their shirts and hopped into the river.

As the sunrays became more concentrated, the water became warmer

"Aah! Haven't had a bath in warm water since days." Said George

"Must be your first-time bathing in a river"

"Nah, we did have a bath in the river before too, in fact, in this river only" replied James

"Ooh, nice, though it might not have been a pleasant experience given that you might be used to long and warm showers in your own fancy cubicles."

"Actually, after the exhaustive journey we had, it was a quite decent wash"

Andrew gave an enchanting smile on this and continued washing the dirt of his body. In some time, the three of them stepped out of the river and dried themselves up by laying under the shed of sunshine.

Wearing their soiled and unwashed clothes, they made their way to the concealed cave.

Romilda waited for them sitting in the far corner of the cave to stay away from the heat. "I have some questions for you Andrew." Said Romilda with a serious face stuck on herself

"Sure, go on"

"This is a bit serious so I don't want you both cracking jokes in the middle of the conversation." Said Romilda pointing towards the demented faces of James and George

"Ok, so do you have any idea about how can we go back to our world because I really do not plan about living here for the rest of my life like a Nomad."

As Andrew just opened his mouth, Romilda blurted out questions one after the other and did not give Andrew to answer them

"How long do we have to stay here, what will it take out of us to go back, can we even get out of here?" asked Romilda

"Lady, you need to at least lend the man some time to answer your question."

"I am sorry, I could not control my feelings anymore." Said Romilda

"I believe that you are anticipated and gravely anxious." Said Andrew analysing Romilda's haphazard state of mind

"I myself don't have a complete answer to your questions and I don't want to feed you with partial information."

"Please help us Andrew, we are not experienced and won't be able to survive in these living conditions any longer."

"Romilda, I think that the witted people of my village, Meraki, can only help you here."

"Ok so take me there!! I cannot stay here any longer."

"Ok, if you want to go so badly, we can start our journey to Meraki tomorrow, but today you will have to relax your mind and body."

"Your bodies are going through a lot of stuff; you need to give your body some time to recover and relax."

"Ok, so we rest today and tomorrow we leave for Meraki early in the morning." Said James

"Yes, you got me right." Said Andrew

After the prominent tensed conversation, they developed an atmosphere of seriousness as the three of them realised that they were actually in an extremely difficult and complicated situation.

The rest of the day wasn't that eventful and they spent it in boredom and anticipation pondering about their journey to Meraki.

As the sun ascended to its maximum calibre, it pointed out lunch time. Lunch was already been prepared by Romilda and James helped her out with a bit. Meanwhile, Andrew and George had dozed off into a cosy corner, a bit deep into the cave.

James woke them up with some small splashes of bone-chilling water, given that they were heavy sleepers and would not wake up casually.

"Lunch time sleepers." Said James

"Yes, but you could have used a comparatively better way to wake us up instead of splashing a whole lot of water on us." Said Andrew softly as he recovered from his sleep to consciousness

"Like you would wake up with some light and mushy touches of my hand on your cheek." Replied James mocking Andrew and George

Meanwhile George stretched his arms and legs trying to get rid of the laziness collected into him due to the long nap he took.

"You might want to stand up and come for lunch too George."

"Yes, I am on my way." Said George as he hugged a huge piece of rock reckoning it was a cushion

"Ouch" moaned George in pain

"That is a rock, not a cushion you buffoon." Said James

Andrew held his stomach tightly as he burst into laughter, soon which led to tears rolling down his cheek

"What is so hilarious in this Andrew, I am a human and I can make mistakes" "And I was half asleep when I, hugged the rock." Said George embarrassed from his actions

"Let me bring it out crystal clear to you; James is just being kind" said Andrew chuckling while throwing out words from his mouth

"What do you mean??" asked George in a confused tone

"I mean that you were not just hugging the rock but you were cuddling the rock." Replied Andrew continuing to laugh even more

George had no reply and moved towards to the lunch place with a weird expression on his face

"Why are you making faces" asked Romilda as she witnessed him coming to the lunch place

"Long story short, George is gravely embarrassed and please don't ask any more questions." Said James

Taking Romilda into a corner, James whispered, "I will narrate the whole incident to you after we have lunch."

"Ok" replied Romilda

They all sat down and started feasting on the freshly cooked fish that was served to them by Romilda

"Andrew, please concentrate on your food and stop chucking or even smiling."

"I feel uncomfortable man, understand!" said George

"Ok, Ok, I will stop and quietly have my food." Said Andrew

"Romilda, are you feeling better now or are you still in that mental state?" asked Andrew interrogated Andrew in a somewhat serious tone

"I am feeling quite alright." Replied Romilda

"Ok, so I think that that it is the right time to bring this up"

"Bring up what" asked James bewildered from Andrew's statement

"Yes, I didn't inform you about this right after we talked today morning as I wanted you to get a mental relief."

"Now that you are feeling better, I must inform you that..."

"That what Andrew??"

"That the route to Meraki is not every one's cup of tea to get through."

"Yes, but you know the route so what is the issue here??"

"Not in that sense; I mean that the route is drenched in a pool of dangers and I can't guarantee that we all will reach there safe and sound."

"So how did reach here, into the jungle?"

"I know magic so I could it wasn't that of a challenge for me to reach out here."

"Yes, so you can help us travel through!" said Romilda

"Of course, I will help you guys to travel through the jungle"

"But, still travelling through is an extremely tedious, difficult and hazardous job"

"Andrew, it is fine; we all are quite grown up and we will stick to you and obey all your instructions so that we stay safe."

There was a long deafening and scary silence until Andrew spoke up.

"Listen, I can just warn you but the decision is yours" "If you actually want to risk your lives for this, then I don't mind taking you to Meraki"

"Yes Andrew, everything will be fine if you think positively and only if we stay careful and aware the whole time."

"Ok, then the plan remains the same; we leave tomorrow after breakfast for Meraki" said Andrew

Ending the conversation they ate their food in a long non defeated silence. The day ended soon and all of them went to sleep preparing their bodies for a rough day ahead.

Andrew had been up before the sun, and prepared for carrying water and some fish as food.

Meanwhile, Romilda, James and George slept peacefully.

"Come on guys, big day ahead; wake up" shouted Andrew in hope of waking them up as soon as possible

The three of them lazily opened their eyes and stretched themselves to escape the lethargy gained over time from their long sleep.

"Might be the last time you slept so peacefully" said Andrew

"Andrew, I do not know about them but I am panic-stricken only because of your warning; please don't make it worse" said George as he stood up to have breakfast

They were served cranberries and some apples which Andrew managed to find in the jungle.

"Start packing up your stuff as soon as you are done with your breakfast"

"Not much time left in our departure towards Meraki"

"Yes, I have already packed up some supplies in the bag that you gave me for the journey"

"Romilda and George; make sure that you take the stuff, that will be useful for you and all of us" said James

As they had their breakfast, Romilda and George rushed towards the river to fill some empty water bottles given to them by Andrew for the journey.

"Feels like I haven't been to Meraki for ages; if we make it there, there will be a lot of stuff for you guys to see" said Andrew as he took a final check for all the stuff he wanted

Romilda and George arrived to the cave in a hurry as the times for them to leave struck down its way in.

"So is everyone ready with the stuff that will be essential for the little trip we are going to take?" asked James

"Yes, unless our predictions go wrong" replied Romilda

"Ok, that is fine; so is everyone good to go?"

Everyone gave a slight nod

"I may take the pain of reminding you that I will be leading you to Meraki so please do listen to me and don't make decisions on your own"

"Keep a sharp tool with you in the pockets of your bags so that it comes in handy as a weapon for all of you"

"It will be enough to fight minor hazards"

"The way to Meraki is haphazard so there is a considerable amount of chance that one of you might fall apart from the group"

"So, stick together or else the jungle will swallow you alive and your bodies and lives will not be found by anyone"

"Ok, Andrew, now let us start moving or else it will be dark and as difficult as ever for us to identify the route to Meraki"

After Andrew finished with his seemingly never-ending set of instructions, they started moving towards the North.

It was early morning but the sunlight was more concentrated than usual days.

They were wearied out in the initial part of the journey because the sun sucked the energy out of them and left them thirsty for water.

"Andrew how long will we have to walk for??" asked George

"Frankly, it will take a couple of hours to reach there."

"It has been no time since we started walking and we all are all out of energy already"

"I think we will have to rest somewhere; maybe near a tree or somewhere you know Andrew"

"Not near a tree for sure; I rested near a tree and you found me the condition that you are well aware of"

"So what do we do then??"

"We will have to stop near a river" "I know, a place where we can find one but it is substantially far away so you guys will have to walk faster"

Soon, they found themselves fighting their physical limits thriving for rest

Romilda crouched and her legs had stopped working. It felt as if the life was sucked out of her

"Come on girl, the river is not so far apart"

"Here, have some water"

Andrew handed over a bottle of water to her, hoping she could get rid of her disturbing thirst and some amount of hunger

They continued walking until they Andrew stopped mid-way.

He pointed towards the pool of mud.

"Look at this" said Andrew in a momentous tone

"What the heck is that!"

"Bears, these are the footprints a bear you don't want to fight"

"Keep your senses sharp and don't think about fatigue or else it will grasp you faster"

"There is a tendency that when you find the footprints of an animal, it is somewhere around you" said Andrew in an alarming tone

"Isn't there any other route that we can take??" asked James out of terror

"I might disappoint you here James; this is the safest, yet extremely dangerous, most reliable and the most used route to reach Meraki" replied Andrew

"Now let's keep moving or else, the time will be not so far when, you will be so weary that you will fall to the ground"

The four of them kept walking without saying a word, trying not to trigger some animals which might result as a danger for them.

The silent noises of the insects and slight groans that were audible to them were enough to make them aware of their surroundings

As they continued walking, they found that the ground was not solid anymore and they could feel mud on their feet.

This made their job way more tougher as the mud would stick to their feet, causing them to itch and make their feet furthermore heavier

"It feels like my feet will fall off in some time"

"Keep going, this is a good sign"

"What, the mud is a good sign!!" exclaimed George

"Yes, as it indicates the presence of water in the nearby area"

After wandering around for some more time carrying the heavy load of restlessness and fatigue, they finally reached a river.

However, it wasn't the river where they were the last time. This one was more violent than the previous one.

It would be safe to say that a person who goes into its depth, would surely struggle heavily to come out of its wrath

"Here we are, take your spots for resting; we won't be lying around here for long so be quick in whatever you want to do."

James went to the river and kneeled down and buried his hands into the soil so that he could avoid toppling over into the river. He dipped his whole head into the low and raging river. His head remained into the river for a good time until he was out of breath.

"The river is rampant but the water is revitalizing and cool."

"You might consider having a dip too"

"I am good; might just sprinkle some water on me" replied George

Andrew was busy sorting his stuff out in his magical bag and Romilda lay down on a bed of leaves, with full energy in herself in the shed of a tree.

Some time passed by as they caressed their body with water and shed.

"Time to go; come on stand up guys or else it will be dark soon." Said Andrew

James had caught on to a plenty of energy and already was ready with his backpack on his back.

"George and Romilda might have fallen asleep" said James

"Yes, you go wake up Romilda and I will wake up our heavy dozer George." Said Andrew

James managed to wake up Romilda in a push or two complementing with some wake up calls.

Andrew tried his best to wake up George by giving him some vigorous pushes and some blaring calls but all his efforts went into vain.

"James, have you managed to get Romilda up??"

"Yes, she is awake"

"I might require your help here waking up this sloth"

"Only water wakes him up Andrew, get some cold water from the river and throw on him"

Andrew filled a bottle full of freezing river water and emptied it completely on George's face.

George was startled and woke up with a jerk.

"Good morning kiddo; time to move" said Andrew

"You guys don't let me get some rest properly" moaned George

"We don't have time for this; get your bag and start moving with us or else we might leave you behind"

Without wasting anymore time, George grabbed his bag-pack and stood up in a matter of seconds on hearing Andrew's statement

"That is quite impressive for idle and inactive guy like you" said Andrew as he started moving in to the jungle again

"What do you mean by that??"

"I think that the statement speaks clearly for itself" replied Andrew

George frowned but continued moving with him. After some time, Andrew buried his hand into his bag-pack pulling out a long piece of parchment and a bottle of water.

He let one or two drops to fall on the parchment and handed the bottle of water to Romilda.

Soon the parchment magically expanded to reveal a map "Wooahhh!! What is that??"

"It is a map George, which is clearly enchanted or something; can't you tell by the looks of it" said James

"Indeed, you are right James; this map is magical" "It shows the way to Meraki from your current position in simple words George"

Romilda, being closest to Andrew joined him in examining the map.

"We will have to move towards North-East direction I guess" said Romilda

"Yes, you are right and the North-East direction will be that way" said Andrew

George also had a look at the map out of curiosity.

"Romilda, how can you read such a complicated map??"

"Because I actually paid attention in Geography lessons" replied Romilda

Andrew chuckled on hearing this

"Why is it that George is always the one who gets embarrassed the most" said Andrew

"Yes because he does stuff like that" replied James

"Let's not start a conversation about me right now; that can be done later in the day"

"I reckon we do have something more important to do; don't we" said George

"That's right, we can talk about it before going to sleep" said Andrew trying to tease George

They proceeded towards the North-East direction.

As they proceeded further, the jungle seemed to be thickening visually.

It also felt as If the level of the mud and the sand had risen up.

Some of the spots on the land would soak their legs into the sand or the mud, making it harder for them to walk normally.

"Feels like we are walking in a pool, but instead of a real pool, it is just a bunch of sand and mud" said James

"I bet that when I will reach home, the first thing that my mom will tell me is to clean by feet"

"They stink like poop" said George

"Don't waste your energy talking kiddo" said Andrew

"How is talking a waste of energy??" asked George

"Hey, who has lived here for longer, you or me"

"You of course"

"Yes so I don't talk by opinions, I talk by my experience" said Andrew

Andrew began to give a slight smirk to Romilda. Romilda knew almost immediately about Andrew's bluff to keep George silent.

"Imagine, this is the easiest and the most manageable route to reach Meraki yet so tedious for you"

"We are not even half way near Meraki and fortunate enough to not encounter anything unusual and concerning till now"

"Not many people survive until they reach this point" said Andrew

"Oh wow!!, that helps a lot in boosting up my confidence Andrew"

"You might like to STOP scaring us with facts and statistics or by being brutally honest" said George shooting his words of irony and sarcasm towards the old-aged

Andrew

"Those are some heavy words and sentences you are using on me George" said Andrew

"More of a need"

Andrew kept quiet for the next few moments as the journey towards Meraki continued.

"Can we stop for a quick break Andrew??" asked Romilda, standing with her hands on her knees showing that she was wearied out.

"Can we take some more rest??" asked Romilda

"I am afraid, I will have to disappoint you here as there no place you can actually sit and rest around here"

"It is also going to be dark soon; might as well consider walking a bit and then we will be in a part of the jungle where I might recognize a spot where you can rest"

"It will be quite dark by that time soon"

"We haven't had any food also Andrew; will need some energy to walk" said James

"Yes, you can just take some fruits in your bags and munch on them while walking" replied Andrew

"Ok, I will manage walking a bit more" said Romilda

They took some food out of their bags on which they could munch on while walking.

Their bag packs were soaked in sweat and so were they. They also had a lot of traces of leaves and mud on them.

As they walked further, they could hear a slight animal like groan.

The sound deepened as they continued walking carrying some amount of exponentially growing fear in their hearts.

"What is that noise?" asked James

"I don't exactly know what it is but might just say that it is definitely not a good sign"

"Keep your eyes and ears open; you don't know what will strike you when and where in here" said Andrew in a profound, deep and a serious tone indicating that something not pleasurable might take place in a few moments

"What do we do, just keep walking or try to hide??" asked George

"Can you find any hiding spots here except for beneath the mud where you won't be able to breath!!" Said James

"Keep it down guys"

"Whatever it is can also have ears and we do not want to attract any unwanted attention towards us" said Romilda

Their hearts pounded as their feet started walking faster trying to escape the spontaneous fear and anxiety.

Something jumped out of a tall tree into the bushes; at least what it seemed like.

"What was that?" asked Andrew

"We have no idea" replied James on behalf of all three of them

"Let me go check" said James

"No! I can't let you go there" said Andrew

James had already started moving towards the bush ignoring Andrew completely

He pulled out the knife that they kept for situations like this and held it tight in his right hand.

Before he could reach over, Andrew came over and pulled.

"What are you trying to do??" asked Andrew

"I told you to listen to me and do what I say"

"Andrew, we will have to go check anyways, let's not delay this anymore"

"You are not going alone, I am coming with you" said Andrew

"Ok, come then"

They both walked towards the bush and Andrew cautiously cut through some of the leaves to only reveal a broken egg.

"What is it??" asked Romilda

"Nothing, just the end of a harmless and an innocent creature"

"What do you mean??" asked Romilda out of confusion

"It's an egg, which is now broken" said James

"Ok, any reason to stop though??"

"Absolutely not!! It's a broken egg" said George

Before they could get their legs back to work, a robust feeling of fear and terror-struck James

"I am not scaring you guys, but stay aware"

"What is your reason to say this??" asked Andrew

"I have a feeling that something terrible is going to happen"

Soon everyone felt silent, unknown whether they were silent because of fear or James' words which eventually lead to the pool of fear too.

Gushes of winds passed by as they stood there, without any movement.

"Can we move now??"

"I am getting terrified now, feels as if my heart just jumped out of my body out of anxiety" said George who was gradually becoming the first victim of trepidation among them

"I don't know why I was silent for such a long moment; felt as if my mind had completely shut down" said Romilda holding her head tightly

"I felt the exact same thing Romilda, it felt as if someone was controlling my mind" said James

"What did you just say James?" asked Andrew hesitantly

"What did I say" said James out of confusion.

"Why are you acting weirdly Andrew?"

"Just answer my question" screamed Andrew

"I said that it felt as If someone was controlling my mind" said James

"No, No, No, this can't be good at all for all of us" said Andrew

It seemed like fear spread in Andrew's mind like a virus which was visible on his face.

"What's the matter with you Andrew" asked Romilda

"Start running, Start sprinting as fast as you can" said Andrew

After saying some more of unclear sentences Andrew started hurtled across the forest.

Romilda, George and James were too confused and too blank to make decisions on their own. Soon they were following Andrew blindly without getting any of the answers to the numerous questions in their mind.

"Why are we running Andrew!!" screamed James

"Don't ask any questions; just keep following me" screamed back Andrew

They kept sprinting with the all the power they had. Andrew came to a quick stop soon and so did Romilda, James and George.

They all just fell to the ground as the vigorous running that they had just done had sucked all the energy out of them and fatigue took all over their mind.

"Why did we run??"

"Were you just scared of a broken egg Andrew??" asked James while he was catching his breath

"Wait a moment" said Andrew

Andrew was taking deep breaths in and releasing them slowly indicating that he was trying to relax his body.

After he was done he gulped down some water and washed his face with some of the water.

"Would anyone like some water??" asked Andrew

"No, already had it" said Romilda

"We just want to know why did you run from there!!" said George

"Let me bring this out in the clear Andrew" "I am not a lion-hearted person and I get scared extremely easily so if this all was just a joke, it was not funny at all"

"I almost threw up while running out of annoyance and fear" said George

"Why were you annoyed??" asked James

"I am not athletic too and do not enjoy sprinting this much at once after freaking walking for several miles"

George seemed as if he was mentally disturbed and did not want any further disturbance to his body or mind in any way possible.

Meanwhile Andrew still lay taking in deep breaths ignoring all of the questions that the rest three of them were shooting towards him.

They waited for a minute or two so that Andrew could come back to his conscious and answer them.

Andrew soon stood up and started talking finally.

"Yes, George I am sorry but this was not a joke at all" "There was a lot of danger there so I had to run" said Andrew still sounding a bit out of breath

"What type of danger are you talking about??" asked James

"Salazars" replied Andrew in a low and serious tone

"What are Salazars?"

"Those are magical creatures which roam around in this part of the jungle with colossal bodies which are filled to the brim with strength"

"But how did you know that one of them was present there without spotting any one of them??" asked James

"Was just coming to that; Another thing about Salazars is that they have this individual quality that they can easily take over someone's mind leading them to do whatever they wish them to do"

"Remember, the moment when we just went speechless for a minute there and only George spoke up to break the silence"

"Yes"

"That was because they did not take over George's mind so he was able to do what he wanted to but if we wanted to move or speak something we weren't able to because our minds had blacked out"

"Tell me now, did you want to be around creatures like this who could have possibly feasted on your flesh in a matter of seconds." Said Andrew

"Yes you did the right thing" said James

"And we thank you for that" said Romilda

"Yes I am truly grateful to you Andrew" said George in a fearful tone "Just one more question to you, if you don't mind Andrew"

"Yes go ahead"

"Are these the most terrible and hazardous creatures in this jungle" said Andrew

"Please tell me they are; if they are not I am surely done for good in this haunted forest" said George

"There are definitely much more dangerous creatures than Salazars in this jungle"

"In fact Salazars are only 50 percent of what some other creatures in this jungle have in them"

"Now that's a terrifying comparison" said Romilda

"Wait guys, can you hear that??" said James

"Hear what??" asked Romilda "There is nothing to hear James, stop messing around with us now" said George

"No, I can also hear something"

"Are those Salazars Andrew??" asked James

"I also feel the same James; I reckon those are Salazars" said Andrew

Andrew pulled all of them into a small and a concealed place where they could hide.

It wasn't the best place to hide as it was a bunch of big ricks covered with leaves. Andrew contemplated for a moment or two and then put his hand into his bag pulling out a lustrous glass vile of an orangish-red liquid.

"Everyone drink this" said Andrew

"What is this, Andrew??" asked James

"This will prevent the Salazars to take over your mind, this is horribly bitter so you might consider diluting it in some water and then consume it" said Andrew handing over the vile to James after consuming some it himself.

"How is this drink going to prevent that in any way??"asked George

"This is known as magic in our world George; now don't ask stupid questions and hurry up!!"

"Will we have to hide in here till they all go away??" asked Romilda

"I do think so but I really don't think that they are planning to go away soon given that they can easily sense human presence" said Andrew

"If you take an estimate, how many Salazars might be there outside waiting to feast on us??" asked James

"If I go by the sounds and the abundance of these nerve-wrecking creatures in this particular area, they might be around 4-5" said Andrew

"And how many will we be able to take down if they see us and we have to fight them?"

"If all of us work extremely hard then too hardly we will be able to only weaken one by some amount" said Andrew

"We don't have any proper weapon to defend ourselves from one of them" said George

"True, now let's keep quiet" "Let me pay attention to their noises or else I will never be able to figure out whether they have left or not" said Andrew

James' curiosity also arose at the moment and he pinned his ear to the surface of one of the 4 rocks behind which they were taking cover to listen to the noises made by Salazars.

"Typical Salazars for sure" said Andrew

The noise of grunting and groaning was now audible to all of them clearly which just added to the amount of consternation mounting up in their heads and hearts.

"These sound a bit different from the noise that we heard in the place from where we ran" said James

"Yes, they sound a bit distinct from them to me too" said Andrew

"Are you sure these are the same creatures Andrew??" asked James

"Yes, I am sure that these are Salazars but I think these ones are not grown up ones; these sound like they are young" replied Andrew

"How do we verify??" asked Romilda

"By looking I guess" said George

"Are you dumb George; what if we go to have a look and end up becoming their dinner" said Romilda

"You are right Romilda" said Andrew

"But how does it even matter that the creatures outside are grown up or baby Salazars?" asked George

"It matters a lot" "Baby Salazars are extremely friendly towards human but as they grow up they start hating humans" said Andrew

"Why is that though??"

"I haven't done complete research on Salazars George that I would know every single detail about them" said Andrew out of frustration

"There is one way we can know whether they are Baby Salazars or grown-up ones without putting anyone of us to risk" said Andrew

"And what method would that be??" inquired James

"We still do have one or two apples right"

"Yes we do" replied Romilda

"Ok, hand me one" said Andrew

Romilda took off her bag and handed the whole bag to Andrew. Andrew dug his hands in to grab an apple

"Are you hungry Andrew??" asked George

"No!! this is not for me" "Why did you bring George along with you here James and Romilda"

"We didn't have a choice; the prophecy didn't ask us whether who all wanted to come and just sucked us in and dropped us here" said Romilda

"I wish you had a choice" said Andrew

"Listen, baby Salazars love apples but the grown up ones just hate them" "I will chuck them out from this hole and we will see if any Salazar is attracted to it or not" said Andrew

"I must say Andrew; you are quite witty" said James

"Thanks for the appreciation James but let's get some work done now" said Andrew

Andrew cleaned the apple of some surface dust and let it slide through the whole out in the open

"Now we wait and watch"

The apple lay there undisturbed for a couple of minutes

"Andrew, no Salazar is coming towards the apple" said James

"I think we will have to throw some more"

Andrew dug his hand again into the bag and pulled out 5 apples this time sliding each one after the other through the whole.

They waited for some more time in hope that some Salazars would notice and attract towards the apples only to feast on them.

"There is no result Andrew; shall we stop waiting for them??" asked James

"Patience is the key; they take some time to sense the apples in their surroundings and inspect them first before coming near to them or consuming them" said Andrew

The kept waiting in the hot room with the covering of rocks on the sides finished by a roof of some banana leaves.

In some seconds they could hear some footsteps and the growing noises of Salazars. In a matter of seconds, they could 6 gigantic green coloured feet with long and uncleaned nails covered in mud near the apples they dropped.

"Yes, these are baby Salazars" "We can go outside now; there is no need to stay hidden" said Andrew

"Are you sure that they won't harm us in any way Andrew?" asked George

"No George, we are good to go" replied Andrew

He started tearing apart the leaves above their head and climbed up a moist rock. James followed Andrew and climbed out too. Then came Romilda. George was the last one to come out of the cover due to fear and anticipation.

He gently landed his feet on the dirt and let his eyes look up to the tremendous creatures in front of him.

In spite of being just baby Salazars they were colossal in with an estimated height of 14 feet and their tale alone was 6 feet long. Their bodies were green in colour and their tails beheld golden spikes which reflected in their eyes as they gazed in marvel and disbelief. Their face was covered in golden and brown hair and seemed as if these creatures were a combination of lions and alligators.

They gave out a loud roar as they saw all of them and George fell down with the noise of their roar alone with James and Romilda taking a step back.

"Don't be scare guys, these are extremely friendly and won't hurt you in any way" said Andrew

The three of them still did not step forward and went a step further again.

Meanwhile Andrew had started caressing one of the Salazars by its cheek and soon mounted on it.

"See, they do absolutely no harm to you and are so-so friendly" said Andrew

James now gathered some will and came closer to another one of the Salazars.

He let his right hand gently slide through the Salazar's neck once. Soon James got comfortable with it and mounted one too.

"Romilda, George, Andrew is right, these are extremely friendly; won't do anything to you." Said James

In some time Romilda had also managed to take over one but George still lay on the ground looking up in the sky towards the Salazar and still letting fear run through his veins on seeing the colossal creatures.

Andrew approached George and helped him stand up. Then he pulled him towards one of the Salazars as George resisted him. He grabbed his hands and let his hand rest on the back of one of them. Then he picked him by the collar and his back and placed him gently on its back.

"Comfortable??" asked Andrew

"I must say Andrew; your way was wrong but your intention was totally right" said George

"Thank you" said Andrew

"Enough of fun Andrew, let's start walking towards Meraki" said George

"We can start the journey but who said that we are going to walk" said Andrew

"Then what will we do, fly??"

"No, we will ride the Salazars" said Andrew

"No way, these creatures will give us a ride" said James

"They will and it will be a good one; a memorable ride for you" said Andrew

Andrew mounted his Salazar again.

"Just start saying the directions; they understand our language" said Andrew

"We don't know the directions" said George

"But I do" said Andrew

"Your Salazars will also follow my command"

"Why??"

"Because I fed them apples" replied Andrew

"Now let's go for a Salazar ride people" screamed out Andrew

"Straight" he shouted as the Salazar took off and started sprinting straight

"This is so much better" shouted out George

"No tiredness and weariness now"

"Yes we will last a lot more than we usually do and these are like our cars for the rest of our journey" said Romilda

"Who said that??" "We will have to leave them as soon as they become drowsy" said Andrew

"So enjoy them to the fullest until an hour or two if we are lucky enough"

"No problem, at least they are saving us a lot bunch of precious time" said Romilda

They rode for a long time. It felt like a good 1 and a half hour to them until the Salazars started slowing down.

Andrew soon instructed them to stop and then he descended from the Salazar's back.

"Come on guys; this is the farthest they can bring us" said Andrew

Romilda and James descended soon enough too but George was fast-asleep.

Andrew slapped him gently on the cheek a couple of times until he woke up and listened.

"Hey, you have to get off the Salazar now" said Andrew

George clumsily got off its back and landed on the floor again.

"How can you possibly fall asleep when the Salazar was moving so much?" asked James

"That is his talent that we have recently discovered James" said Andrew

"He can sleep anywhere and anytime until he gets a place to put his lazy bottom on"

Romilda and James chuckled meanwhile George stood there recovering to his conscious clueless of what was going on.

The sun had already gone down and the sky had worn a dark mask scarce of any light.

"It is too dark to continue walking now; we will have to stay somewhere around here for the night and we will continue our journey tomorrow" said Andrew

"Ok, but where?"

"That is the part we will have to figure out" replied Andrew

"Let's not waste any time now; start searching for someplace where we can sleep"

"I can't see anything in the dark; how will we even find a place??" asked George

"You will have to manage; that is what I am doing"

The began the desperate quest for a place to rest in for rest of the night.

"One little piece of advice for you people; there are caves everywhere in this jungle but they are just concealed"

"Think creative and search places which are hideous and you will definitely find a place" said Andrew

"Everyone spread out in different directions and search for a place" "It will be much faster that way" said James

"All of them dispersed in different direction, all in the radius of nearly 50 metres. James went into the check whether any leaves might have covered some places to stay in.

Meanwhile Romilda, accompanied by George had headed into the thick woods to find some wood to light a fire.

Andrew was also searching for a place or material to build a place.

Several minutes passed by but they could not locate any place where they could possibly spend the rest of the night.

James came out of the bushes and approached Andrew.

"Could not find anything Andrew"

"Same, I also could not find a single place; only one option left now"

"And what would that be??" asked James

"Build a roof" replied Andrew

"We will have to build a place for ourselves"

"Let's wait for Romilda and George and then we will start the work"

Romilda soon came towards Andrew and James carrying a whole pile of dry wood for the fire.

"Here is the wood" said Romilda as she dropped it gently on the ground

"Where is that lethargic friend of yours??" asked Andrew

"He was just right behind me"

"But he has not come Romilda" said James

"He might have just tangled up somewhere" "I will just go and have a quick look; meanwhile you guys start the work"

"I will be back in a second"

Romilda proceeded into the woods again in search of George.

"Hey George, where are you??" shouted out Romilda in hope of a response of George

She searched a bit deeper and reached the spot from where they picked up most of the wood.

She could find nothing except for the native insects, broken twigs and scattered leaves in the same position she saw them before.

Romilda searched in the surrounding area too to verify whether George is there or not.

She was again disappointed. She started worrying now and rushed back to James and Andrew.

"Guys, I searched for George everywhere but I could not find him anywhere" said Romilda in a worrisome tone

"Did you check everywhere??" asked James

"Yes I did" replied Romilda

"I will go have a look and come back in a moment; you guys stick together and don't go anywhere" said Andrew as he rushed into the woods

Meanwhile James and Romilda stood there waiting for Andrew to come.

In a couple of minutes Andrew approached them.

"Did you find him anywhere??" asked James

"No, I am afraid he is lost or been…"

"been what Andrew??" asked Romilda

"Been picked up" replied Andrew

"What!!! How can someone just kidnap George without him screaming" asked Romilda

"Romilda, keep it low; these are situations in which you need to keep your mind as cool as possible and think wisely

"What do we do now??" asked James

"We will have to wait until the morning so that we can look for clues around the place which will help us find him" said Andrew

"What do we do until then??"

"You sleep"

"Andrew, what are you talking about; I can't sleep with my best friend in such a grave trouble"

"You will have to understand the same thing I told to Romilda James; we don't have any other option"

James and Romilda were convinced.

They went to bed in the shelter that James and Andrew made together while they all were gone.

They used all of the wood to give support to the pile of leaves they used as a roof.

All of them slid under the cover and soon started trying to sleep.

But the worry of George and the sound of insects in the silence of the haunted jungle didn't let them sleep.

Disturbing thoughts encroached their mind no matter how hard they tried to keep them away.

However they all managed to catch a nap which eventually helped them dissolve some tiredness.

Soon the sun paved its way up in the vast sky as the three of them got the indication to wake up from their sleep.

"Guys wake up, we need to go searching for George" said Andrew

James and Romilda were fast awake.

"Just eat whatever you have while you are walking if you feel hungry; not going to stop anywhere for breakfast or anything like that" said Andrew

The all had a sip of water, washed their faces with the leftover water.

"Romilda, I want you to guide us to the exact spots to where you and George went, specifically where George went"

"Ok, I will take you there" replied Romilda

"But, before that I you might consider answering my question"

"Yes, go ahead and ask your question"

"Did George go away from you anytime while you were busy collecting wood"

"No, he was helping me pick It up because it was too heavy for me" said Romilda

"Ok, try taking me through the exact path you took to go into the woods and come back from the woods" said Andrew

Romilda started walking into the thick part of the jungle with numerous trees everywhere and dry leaves scattered all over the jungle floor

"Here is the path we took" said Romilda

Andrew started examining the path for distinct type of footsteps. Initially there were only two different types of footsteps which were leading into the woods which were of Romilda and George.

In a span of few metres a third type of footstep was visible to them.

"Look at this; notice how all these types of footsteps are always behind your and George's footsteps meaning whoever it was, was following you people" said Andrew

"Yes, they are deviating from the path that Romilda takes back to Andrew and these lines mean that George was dragged in that direction only" said James

"Oh my god; that might have hurt George so much"

Andrew took some steps further until he stepped on a bottle with a type of liquid he was familiar with.

He bent down grasping the bottle in his hand opening its lid, he smelled the liquid.

Andrew was struck with a wave of dizziness and instantly closed the glass bottle's lid immediately recognizing the liquid that lay in it.

"Romilda, the dragging didn't hurt George one bit" said Andrew in a serious tone

"What do you mean Andrew??" asked James

"George had fallen unconscious before he was dragged by the person" replied Andrew

"How do you know that??" asked Romilda

"That is because, this bottle has been found just some distance away before the lines showing that George has been dragged started" said Andrew while flashing the bottle to Romilda and James

"What is that bottle supposed to mean??"

"This bottle has a liquid which makes you fall unconscious for a certain time"

"Might keep that in my pocket" said James

"Why do you want to keep that James??" asked Andrew

"So that we can used it against any person or a creature that might be hazardous to us" replied James

"Ohh, that is extremely smart of you James" said Andrew

James placed that bottle carefully in his bag in a side-pocket.

"Let's follow these lines; they might lead us somewhere" said Andrew

The three of them started walking on the path of the lines.

The lines continued to a long extent; to such lengths that they were tired after walking for such a long distance

Andrew pulled out the map to look at whether they were heading towards a landmark.

Soon, the lines ended and they were left to the shore of a river

"Andrew, the lines have ended here; what do we do now??"

"I think that George might be carried on a boat from here" said Andrew

"Now, from where will we arrange for a boat??" asked Romilda out of frustration

"I am thinking on that bit too Romilda" said Andrew

"I think we will just have to follow the river bank until we find a way to travel through the river" said James

"Nice suggestion James"

"But in which direction do we start walking??" asked Romilda

"We will have to walk in the direction in which the river is flowing" said James

"Yes you are right" said Andrew

The three of them started walking in the direction of the flow of the river

They kept walking until they got nearly halfway through the length of the river.

The sky suddenly changed its colours.

Black clouds had dominated the sky which did not allow even a speck of light to reach towards the ground.

It was as dark as midnight and soon there was lightning in the sky.

It started raining cats and dogs.

With the sky blaring thunder and roaring fear grew among Romilda, James and Andrew

"It has started raining; where do we take cover Andrew??" asked Romilda

"Just use a tree; will not protect you from getting wet but will surely delay it substantially" replied Andrew

The three of them sat under three random trees with the most density of leaves so that they could avoid maximum amount of water reaching them.

In some time, the intensity of the rain increased and so did that of the thunder.

It seemed as if the sky was calling out for a war against the mankind.

James could hear a slight noise of a crying woman in the midst of the thunder.

"Can you hear that Andrew??"

"Hear what??" asked Andrew

"I can hear someone cry out"

Andrew started looking everywhere to locate a person. To his surprise it was Romilda who was crying.

Several drops of water were rolling down her cheek as she wept.

"What happened Romilda??" asked James

There was absolutely no answer from Romilda.

"Speak something Romilda" said Andrew

"I feel guilty" moaned Romilda

"But why; you haven't done anything wrong" said Andrew

"I should have paid attention; if I would have, George would have still been with us"

"And now here we are, in middle of nowhere; not knowing about how much pain George must be going through" said Romilda

"It is not your fault at all Romilda; how could you have known that George was being taken away when the person who took him did it in such a silent way" said James trying to console Romilda

"Yes, James is right; now stop feeling guilty about it and keep your mind as calm as possible"

James offered some water to Romilda who still beheld guiltiness and gloominess on her face. Romilda gulped some of the water.

"Are you fine now??" asked James

Romilda gave a slight nod making James convinced that she is fine.

In some time the rain and the thundering stopped making the sky as clear as ever.

The sunshine now scattered in the sky making it much brighter in the day.

"Come on guys; the rain has stopped and we need to start moving," said Andrew

James and Romilda picked up themselves and started following Andrew.

"Hey Andrew, look at this"

"What is it?" inquired Andrew

James pointed towards the ground showing off a big dent into the soil of the river bank.

"What does this seem like Andrew??" asked James

"I am sure, this is the print of boat" replied Andrew

"Does this mean that we stop here because I can see a waterfall ahead" said James

"Yes, you are right" "The boat would not have gone any further from here" said Andrew

"There are some footprints here too Andrew" said Romilda pointing towards the wet soil from the rain.

"The person is not too far from us" said Andrew examining the footprints carefully

"How do you know about that??" asked James

"It has been several hours since George has been missing; if the person might have taken him away then, these footprints would have been destroyed by the rain for sure"

"And even this void would have been washed away by the fast flow of the river"

"Whoever, it was who took George is not too far and might be somewhere in the jungle only" said Andrew

"This means we will need to be as quick as possible or he might get out of our reach soon" said James

"Yes, let's start walking" said Romilda

They started chasing the footprints with the maximum pace they could walk with. In some time, they reached a spot where the footprints had become that of two people, revealing the entry of a second person.

"Andrew, other pair of footprints" said James

"These are George's footprints for sure" said Romilda

"How do you know??" asked Andrew

"George has the exact same shoes that have; I recognize his footprints because mine match these ones" said Romilda

On saying this Romilda stepped in front of James and Andrew proving them her point.

"This means that George is no more unconscious but is not walking by his wish"

"The person who took him has a weapon of some kind for sure"

"He might be threatening George"

"Come on walk faster; but remember; keep your pocket knives in handy" said Andrew

In some time the footprints had ended as they were exposed to a huge rock in front of them.

"The footprints end here; and a rock is here" said James

"What could this mean??"

Andrew gently placed his hand on to the moist and cold surface of the rock sliding it across its body to get evidence of where the person might be.

He soon removed his hand from the surface of the rock and let his ear push against it.

He listened carefully until his ears could detect some slight sound coming from the mere inside of the rock.

"He is inside" said Andrew

"George is inside??" asked James

"Don't speak loudly; whisper"

"Yes George is inside and so is the person who took him"

"Let's remove the rock then" said Romilda

"Don't act dumb Romilda; the person who has taken away George will get alerted and might be ready to attack before we would be removing the rock"

"We will have to think about something better and more intelligent" said Andrew

"Andrew, if we wait too long, something might happen to George"

"We don't have time to think at all" said Romilda

Terror and anxiety ran through their spine like a wave.

The tension of the moment rose as their minds struggled to find an answer to the difficult situation.

"Andrew, I can't think of anything; can you??" asked James

"No, my mind has also gone blank"

"Yes, so instead of wasting time, let's remove this rock and save George"

"No, James there has to be a better way"

"As of now this is the only way that we have; all we can do is delay this but not find an alternative for going in"

Andrew sounded convinced and he nodded.

He ordered James and Romilda to hide behind the side of wall of the rock till he completely opens pushes the rock out.

Andrew went on and started to push the rock until James stopped him to do so midway

"There is another way you can remove the rock"

"What is that??" asked Andrew

"Don't push the rock; bury your hand into the these two dents and pull it so that you have the rock's cover and we can go in as soon as you are done"

"That is smart" said Andrew

"I will do the removing of the rock so that as soon as it is removed you can immediately take care of the situation inside" said James

"That's right James; there's some brains you got" said Andrew complementing James on his thinking

James readily stood in front of the rock beginning to hug it so that his hands could reach over the dents. He grasped the rock by the dent and started pulling with full power. In some seconds the huge rock started to slide over as the sunshine drifted into the darkness of the cave-like structure on the other side of the rock.

The sunshine reflected over George's face which was covered in mud.

He was tied with metal chains onto a chair.

Andrew carefully observed the place and noticing no one except for George, he dashed into the dark tunnel.

He clasped the chains and tried to break them open in order to free up George.

George was trying hard to speak something but unable due to a cloth tied tightly around his jaw.

Romilda reached over and removed the cloth from George's mouth to allow him to speak.

"Look out Andrew" screamed George.

A person slid behind Andrew with a katana going for an attack on Andrew.

Before the person could swing the katana into Andrew's torso James interrupted the fatal blow grasping his hands and pushing him back into the wall. The person stood and changed his attention to James. He swung his katana into the air attempting to slit open James' throat but James bent down enough to barely miss the sharp surface of the weapon.

He used his pocket knife to make a cut big enough to bring the person on his knees screaming in agony as blood drained from his wound.

"James are you fine??" asked Romilda sounding concerned for James

"Thanks a lot James; you saved my life" said Andrew showing his gratitude towards James

"Nice one mate" shouted out George who was awestruck on seeing James' moves

"Thanks guys; I am fine" replied James

As the four of them started to indulge in a conversation, the person tried standing up, clutching his katana and tried attacking James.

James noticed this which lead to the person ending up with a fist on his nose directly.

The power of the punch by James was such high that he started bleeding and fell unconscious.

"Oooo!!" shouted Romilda

"I must say James; you have got strength with brains" said Andrew complementing James

"Ok let's not have a conversation about the action and let's focus on George here"

James leaned over to give his friend a hug, who was now free from the metal chains.

"How are you George, how did this all happen??" asked James

"Actually I don't remember anything from the last night" "I just remember getting unconscious and the next thing I see is this person with Katana whom I don't know is threatening me to kill me and order me to walk with him"

"Did he mention upon why he was doing this??" asked Andrew

"No, he did not; just gave me two three punches when I asked him who he was" said George who was sounding confused

"So this person hit you for nothing!" said James

"Pretty much yes" replied George

James kicked the unconscious man twice or thrice letting his anger out on him.

"Spare this anger for later James" said Romilda stopping him to go on further before he dies

"Yes don't kill him before we get a chance to let our anger out on this crazy man" said George

"Have you had anything since last night??" asked Andrew

"No, supposedly kidnappers are not kind enough to feed you" "I am starving; might just say I am ravenous and would feast on anything at this point" said George

"Hey have some berries" "Picked them up on the way; they are fresh" said Romilda handing over a handful of berries to George

"So what do we do now Andrew??" asked Romilda

"George is not in the condition of walking right away; we will take today off and continue our journey tomorrow"

"This will give George enough time to rest and time for us to interrogate this lunatic" said Andrew pointing towards the unconscious man.

"Are you fine with that??" asked Andrew

"We are but we don't really matter here; ask Romilda, she is the boss" said James

"You are hilarious James; I am fine Andrew" replied Romilda to James' joke.

"Will we be lying around here for the rest of the day??" asked George

"Yes, that is the one thing this man has done for us" replied Andrew

"Quick question, is this guy going to wake up again??" asked Romilda

"I think that James will be the one who should be answering this question.

"If, I take my strength in account, then this guy might never wake up"

"Nice flexing James; by the way let's take the katana away from him and tie him to the chair using these metal chains" said George

"Nice idea George"

Andrew and James picked up the unconscious man and put him on the chair. Andrew picked up the metal chains from the floor and used them tied them around the chair so that the person could not move If he woke up.

"So now what do we do??"

"We do anything we want"

"Sounds like a plan" said James

"Andrew, so how far are we set back due to this accident??" asked Romilda

"Set back on what??"

"Our journey to Meraki"

"Actually I will have to check the map for that one" said Andrew as he pulled out his map from his bag pack.

He carefully examined the map and gave a slight smile to Romilda.

"What are you smiling for" asked Romilda

"We haven't been set back; instead we have proceeded further in reaching there, it is only that the route has been changed"

"Ohh, that is nice to hear after-all" said Romilda relieved by Andrew's words

"Can we go and have a wash in the river Andrew?" asked George

"No, that is the one thing you must not do"

"The flow of the river is extremely fast and there is a waterfall few metres away"

"I don't want to go and take on the burden to find any of you anymore"

"Got it Andrew" said James trying to stop Andrew to speak anymore

"James and me are right outside just taking a stroll so if you have any work from us then we will be right outside" said George as James and George walked out of the dark tunnel.

"What do you think Andrew??" asked Romilda

"Please can you tell me what to think about??"

"Oh yes, forgot about that; what do you think about this man who is lying unconscious" "Why must he have picked up George out of both of us??" asked Romilda

"I don't have any idea about that; I haven't actually had an inspection of this man" said Andrew

"Might as well just check his pockets for some evidences so that I can answer your questions"

Andrew approached the unconscious man and bent over to reach over to his pockets. He slid his hands into his pockets getting a wet handkerchief out of them.

"Watch out Andrew, that might be used by him to wipe"

"Ok, I figured that out Romilda; no need to gross me out even more"

Andrew sniffed the handkerchief and felt dizzy.

"This is not used for wiping; this is used to make George unconscious" said Andrew

"Oh, yes, that makes sense" added on Romilda

"I reckon, this is all he had on him" said Andrew as he came back on his feet.

"Romilda, let's catch some fresh air"

Romilda and Andrew went outside joining James and George in their stroll.

They all roamed around the jungle, feasting upon some fruits lying around on the floor filling themselves up.

In some moments they could hear the noise of metal making a loud sound from a distance.

"Can anybody hear that??" asked James

"Yes, it is coming from the tunnel"

"I think that man has come back to conscious again" said Andrew

They all ran into the tunnel before they found that the person was successful in escaping.

They reached in the tunnel and heard the person asking for help.

"Who are you people; why did you trap me like this??" asked that man

"We are the people whose friend you picked up last night" said Andrew

"Now tell us, why did you kidnap him and bring him hear??" asked Romilda

"Who are you to interrogate me"

"We are the victim's friends; now speak you evil innocent man or else you will get a fist right back in your face again"

"This time I will not go easy on you" said James

"Like you did the last time" whispered George

"That's right, but I will go even harder this time" whispered James

"I am here to protect this jungle" said the man out of fear

"I can't reveal my identity but I would like to say that I am not a person who wants to harm innocent people in my defence"

"So what did you do to me last night was what??" "I am also an innocent soul; I do not wish on harming anyone" said George

"Yes you tied him up in metal chains; how would you explain that??"

"I said I can't reveal my identity; I have some rules of mine and my place" said the man

"Ok, I suppose you might have a name assigned to yourself"

"Yes I do"

May we know what would that be?" asked Andrew

"My name is David" "Full name!!" shouted James

"David Oliver, David Oliver" screamed the man out of fear

Ok David, now we don't care that you are not allowed to reveal your identity; we want to know who you are and why did you take away George"

"I can answer the second question but not the first one" said David

"Ok, answer whichever question you can" said James out of frustration

"I have been living in the jungle for years and I protect the jungle and its wildlife from invaders."

"I saw this boy roaming around at night and I had never seen him before so I took him away to question him."

"Why did you take him away; you could have questioned him there and then; I don't think that I can believe you" said Romilda

"No, No, this is my hideout and I am supposed to interrogate suspicious people here" replied David who was desperately wanted to clear the confusion in their mind right now.

"Ok, and what people do you work for??" asked James

"I have repeated that multiple times and this is the last time I am telling you this; I cannot reveal my identity to unknown people" replied David

"Tell us where do you come from??" asked Andrew

"I live around here; in one of the villages" replied David

"Which village??" asked Andrew

"I refrain from answering this question of yours" "I assume you are a wise man; I must tell you that there are certain rules by which I must abide or else I will lose my job" said David in hesitation

"Ok, Andrew; I think we have been entertaining him a lot here"

"Let me punch him once more so that he can blurt out something understandable" shouted James

"Calm down James, Meraki also has people who are not supposed to reveal their identity" "I think we should listen to this man" said Andrew

"Wait, did you just say Meraki??" asked David

"Yes, he did; any problem with that??"

"I am not sure whether I am making a mistake by telling this but that is the village I come from??"

"Wait what, you work for the Archade?? Asked Andrew

"Yes, I do work for it" replied David in a shocking tone

"What are you both talking about; Andrew what is Archade??" asked Romilda

"Archade is the village council I am in"

"So do you have the bag that is given to everyone when you join the council??" asked Andrew

"Yes I do have it, it must be lying around deep in the tunnel"

"James, go inside and search for a bag which looks like mine; if you find one, immediately bring it out here" said Andrew

James went deeper into the tunnel. As he walked past several metres of the tunnel, the temperature fell a bit and it felt slightly cooler deep into the tunnel. He spotted a white bag, one like Andrew's hidden behind a rock.

James picked it up and dashed towards the mouth of the tunnel where the rest of them were waiting for him.

"Is this the one which he is talking about??" asked James

"Yes, that is my bag" said David

"I told you, I am not an evil person and work for an institute"

"I will decide that David; Meraki is a famous village and information about Archade can be easily retained through some external sources" "And how hard is it to carry a bag around" said Andrew

As Andrew completed his sentences he started looking into the bag, examining the contents of each and every vile carefully.

"I think, he is harmless James; he has almost the same potions as me, in fact some more advanced than what I have which is a bit unfair" said Andrew as he kept the bag beside David's chair on which he still sat

David's eyes portrayed his anger towards James as he remember the punch that he got in the face from the child as he stared towards James.

"You see kid, you must RESPECT people who are elder to you and think before taking any actions" said David mocking James and trying to make him realise his mistake.

"I am absolutely sorry sir, I punched you in the face and talked loudly in front of you but that was not to disrespect you" "It was all for my friend" said James as he frantically searched for an excuse to justify his actions

"I see, you know the word SIR"

"Let me introduce you to everyone David"

"This is Romilda, George and James" said Andrew as he pointed towards everyone

"I am Andrew Bozila, from Meraki; you must have figured that out and I am a part of Archade" said Andrew as he showed off his bag to him as proof

"These three have come from another world accidentally, called the Earth through a prophecy if I am not wrong and thrive to go back to their world" said Andrew

"I will believe you Andrew; had you not been with them, I would have never believed these are in trouble and are not a danger to the jungle or to any person protecting the jungle" said David as he mocked James again.

"Yes these are innocent lads"

"Can you people consider untying me??; the metal chains hurt a lot" said David as he struggled to stay in the chair with tightly tied metal chains poking him.

"Ohh forgot about that" said James as he proceeded and unclamped the metal chains from David and the chair.

David stretched his arms and got up from the chair.

"Another question, David, I never saw you in the council meetings when I was back in Meraki" "So are you newly appointed into the council??" asked Andrew

"Yes, I joined two weeks ago"

"When were you last in Meraki or specifically a council meeting??" asked David

"I think it might have been in one around an amplete ago" said Andrew

"What is an amplete Andrew??"asked George

"It is a unit for time; like an additional one for the cycles of meetings we conduct at Archade" replied Andrew

"Ohh, that is so cool"

"Let's talk about that later George" "Yes, David, so where were we?"

"Amplete ago; that makes sense because I joined Archade two weeks ago" replied David

"But I need to lodge an application for renewing my items; they are getting expired, some are used up and I don't have the latest potions" said Andrew

"Yes, sure"

"I think that you both can talk about your council in private later" said Romilda

"Let's talk about something that we three can understand too"

"Ok, sure; we don't have a problem with that"

"It is dark outside; I think it is dinner time" "I am starving; haven't had a proper meal since yesterday"

"If you want to eat dinner, I do have some fish but you will have to cook it" said David

"That's great; we have been used to cooking fish now" said Andrew

They began the preparations for their dinner.

James brought a dry wood from inside the cave.

Andrew and David brought in huge logs of trees that they found lying around for making a seating arrangement.

They lit the fire and tossed on some fish with sticks onto the fire.

In a few moments aroma of cooked fish spread through the room.

"That actually smells amazing" said George

"Yes, and there is quite a lot of fish so eat as much as you want to but do have some control or else you might fall sick" said David

All of them grabbed a fish and put it into their mouth.

"That is delectable!!" exclaimed James

"Yes, this is Meraki's special fish"

"Yes, felt like Meraki to me" said Andrew

The room was filled with silence. Everyone was gravely busy in the enjoying the flavour of the fish and did not let a single word spill from their mouth until they were finished with their meal.

"Thanks for that wonderful meal, David; we really appreciate it" said Andrew

"Sir Andrew you don't need to thank me, you are my head in the council"

"Yes but superiority should not stop me from showing my appreciation towards someone" said Andrew

"Do we let the fire keep going??" asked James

"Yes, it will get cold in the night; just let it continue" replied David

"James, close the entrance to the tunnel with the help of George too; the wind might blow out the fire" said Andrew

James and George grabbed the rock and pulled it back in which blocked all of the light that came into the tunnel.

"There will be no light for us in the morning"

"We will push away the rock then; after all we will need to get out of this cave to continue our journey" said Andrew

"Wait, you aren't leaving tomorrow right"

"Yes, in fact we are leaving for Meraki early in the morning tomorrow" said Andrew

"Is that necessary??" asked David

"Yes, these kids need to go back and only the people in Meraki can help them reach back" replied Andrew

"We are already a day late because of this whole accident"

"Why don't you come along with us??" asked James

"Yes, that will be of great help to us and you can also get a break from your job"

"I can't, I still need to look after the jungle and I joined two weeks ago only so I cannot demand a break from them"

"Come on come with us, I can help you get an excuse; after all I am in the highest possible post in the council"

"Don't worry about that"

"Ok, I will come; if you persuade so much" said David

"Great, start packing for whatever you want additionally" "We will be leaving tomorrow early in the morning" said Andrew

All of them started preparing for going to bed, meanwhile David was busy packing for tomorrow.

In some minutes, they all were fast asleep midst the warmth of the cave.

In a few hours some wind squeezed itself in through tiny gaps in the entrance to blow the fire off.

The cave did not have any source of light as darkness spread through it.

In some hours the sun rose and so did David.

He could not see anything but darkness in the morning because the fire had went out and the rock had blocked all the light.

However, tiny specks of light did dance around the cave, they were so less in quantity that they were of minimal help to David's vision.

The morning was frosty. Soon, David grabbed a piece of wood from the pile of wood he stumbled upon.

He tied a leaf around the tip of the wood and lit it.

The sudden fire from the wooden piece startled him as he let his grip onto the torch loose and he soon found it on the floor.

He let it lie on the floor and reached out towards the rock which was closing the entrance.

He pushed it with all the force he had as it slid away from its mean position. In some time, the tunnel had filled with light and warmth came in as the sunrays hit them directly.

"Come on, everyone, time to wake up" shouted out David

He reached out everyone and gave them a shake to wake them up from their tranquil slumber.

All of them woke up. George took some time but surprisingly woke up in some time. "Thanks for waking up everyone David" said Andrew

"My pleasure" replied David

"Everyone clean yourself and freshen up; the breakfast will be ready in some time"

David walked out of the tunnel with James' bag to fill it up with some fruits for breakfast.

He picked up all the fruits, and placed it into the bag after carefully observing them to check whether they would be safe to eat.

In not more than half an hour, he walked back in the tunnel with a bag full of juicy and delicious and tasty fruits.

Meanwhile David was collecting fruits for breakfast, the rest of them went by the river bank to clean themselves. The dust lying on the floor of the tunnel had caught them and changed their colour of skin to deep brown in specific uncovered parts of the body.

They came in and found themselves a beautifully arranged breakfast on a bunch of leaves.

The fresh juice with water dripping from its surface appealed to their eyes and made them substantially hungrier.

"This is ravishing" said George

"I can't believe you did all of this by yourself David; thanks a lot" said James

"No problem people; now let's start feasting on these fruits"

"They are fresh and I have collected the most distinct varieties of them for change of taste and overall nourishment" said Andrew

"Yes, it is visible that there are millions of fruits arranged on this platter" said Andrew

In no time they all were seated around the grand platter of fruits. They began grabbing the fruits which appealed to them and tossed them into their mouth.

"I have collected some for the journey too; they all are in the bag that James gave me"

"Thanks a lot David; you have made our task so much easier and have done so much for us" said Romilda pleased by the heart touching work done by David.

"That is my work Romilda, thanks for the appreciation though"

In some time they winded up with their breakfast and took a quick scan of the tunnel to look for their belongings.

All of them packed up their bag and had them on their shoulders soon. James was struggling to carry the bag full of fruits making his shoulders ache in minutes.

"Let's start moving" said Andrew

"I have another route from which you can reach Meraki faster" said David

"Yes, we are already taking that route, the fastest one right"

"No, recently they have discovered another route to Meraki which is shorter than the previous ones"

"Ok, nice; I guess then we will change the order in which we walk" said Andrew

"David, you lead us; then you three and in the end, me"

"Noted" replied David to Andrew's orders

Andrew handed over his map to David and went behind James, Romilda and George.

They started walking deeper into the jungle and as they walked in, it became more and more dense with bushes and leaves.

They all had to deal with a lot of cutting and clearing out of unnecessary plants which were obstructing them to continue to walk.

They could hear constant hisses, unknown noises of animals and even tiny noises of crickets would jump scare them.

The more resistant the jungle became, more energy it demanded from them and sucked their energy at a fast rate.

In turn they had to keep themselves nourished with fruits, in turn cutting the food supply by a substantial amount.

The only thing that pleased someone was that, the high consumption of fruits, unloaded James' bag considerably making it easier for James to carry their food.

"How harder does it get to walk; if I ever reach home, I will not get up from the bed for two or three days" said George exhausted from the amount of clearing everyone had to do.

"Yes, these bushes and plants will delay the walk quite a lot, this is a new route; barely even used by many people" "Believe me though; this is the best route to Meraki"

"It is fine David" "These kids haven't adapted to the walking thing" said Andrew

"What!! We have been walking and walking since the day we have been here" squeaked Romilda

"Yes, it has been barely a week since you have come" "The natives of this place keep sprinting from one place to the other and follow the same exhaustive schedule for years until the end of their lives" said Andrew

George contemplated the life of the native people and could not help to keep this in.

"So do the people here spend their whole life in walking or travelling on foot??" asked George

"No!! there is a purpose to everything and people are hell bent to achieve that"

"In doing so, we have adapted to the constant mobility via foot making us fitter and faster" said David

"I am sure, Andrew can walk way faster but we both are walking according to your pace"

"Ok, we get it!! The people in our world are lazy and use cars as a medium of travel" said James

"What are cars??" inquired David

"They are mediums of transport which are way faster and comfortable to travel in" replied James

"Still did not get it but leave it for later"

David was the person with the most amount of movement from legs and hands.

He carried a knife, which he used to cut out the obstructions and chucked them away a few metres from them.

In some time they, stopped for rest as they could not walk any further a couple hours straight.

They were drenched in sweat and the constant mobility of legs and hands is like a constant exercise which they need to keep in practise.

They splashed some water on their hot faces to refresh themselves.

They were not hungry as they kept munching on some fruits while they wandered around in the jungle.

"How far is Meraki??" asked George

"I don't have any idea" replied David

"Look at the map and tell"

"The map does not tell the amount of distance left; it just tells the directions"

"Ohh god!!" screamed George

"Hey!! Don't scream like this; there are animals that can be triggered from this annoying noise of yours" Andrew

"Yes, and then they attack you" added on David

"Can you estimate the time it will take for us to reach Meraki??" asked Romilda

"If we walk at a decent pace, then we will reach there till the sun goes to sleep today itself" replied David

"What is a decent pace??" asked James

"The pace that we are walking is slow; we need to walk a bit faster" "A little faster would be considered in the category of decent"

"If I walk faster than this till the sun goes down; I am not even joking at this point, my legs will fall off" whispered James showing his frustration and anxiety.

"You all need to know that, there is some certain amount of distance you will have to cover to reach somewhere"

"And to reach somewhere faster, you will need to walk faster; no harm in bearing some amount of pain for the same" said Andrew

They continued their discussion until they were under the shade for long enough that they could dry off the sweat and get rid of the weird smell of the same.

In some time, they found themselves walking again but this time, all of them were a whole lot quieter.

In some minutes they reached out of the dense jungle and reached over to somewhat barren land.

The land was totally barren with hard soil over it with not a single drop of moisture or a single tree or plant.

Their eyes were so used to the greenery around them that they found their surroundings somewhat bland and the only colours visually available to them were the brown soil and the blue sky. The sky was clear bursting out a bunch of sunlight and did not show any hints of further rain.

The clear land considerably made their way easier as there were plants to be cleared out.

This made them much more efficient in terms of energy usage. However, they were exposed to the sun directly as there were no trees to protect them from the harsh rays.

"Why does it feel like the land we are walking on, has suddenly changed??" asked George

"It has not changed; it is just that this part of the jungle seems to not get enough humidity to supposedly be able to grow any type of trees or even plants." Replied David

"Yes, this area has been talked about in many council meetings" added in Andrew

"I won't complain about this place as the land is way more preferable to walk upon; doesn't suck your leg into the ground" said James

"Yes, that is an advantage we have a decent amount of walking to do in this area until we dive into the greenery again, which will make you extremely thirsty and also hot"

"The sun is scorching hot; you will feel it in some time; I suggest that you walk as fast as you can hear"

"Andrew, you said that the route to Meraki will be full of danger, but till now we haven't tackled any" said Romilda

"Yes, we have been quite lucky till now to not encounter any; doesn't mean that we will not be finding any" replied Andrew

"This part does not have any dangerous creatures of any sort but the distinct weather is dense enough to burn your skin down and making you crave some shade" said And raw

They constantly had to sip water to keep themselves protected from the breath wrenching heat from the sun leading them to finish most of the water they held.

In some time they walked into a relatively greener part with some amount of plants in the area but trees were still scarce to their eyes and they still could not find any source of water to fill their bottles up from.

Sometime later, they walked into the jungle yet again but with scarcity of water and lack of energy.

They tried their luck to find a river or a pond but could not find one.

They had to survive on the juicy fruits to keep themselves hydrated.

They were again into the puddle of never ending liquified soil which sucked them in on every step they took ahead.

"Guys, good job keeping up with my pace; now we need the escape the deadly and gut wrenching wreath of thirst" said David out of frustration

"Hey, don't use such complicated words, I am already having a hard time processing my life"

"If you further load my brain with anything else, it might blast into a zillion minute pieces" said George

"Yes, will try to be normal, but I feel thirsty" said David

"Does anyone have some water??"

"No, not even a single drop; all of it got exhausted on the way from the barren land" replied James

In some time they could do nothing but rest beneath some trees.

James, along with David went on to search for some water, in the nearby area.

He hunted down several fruits but could not find any water.

When he reached over to the place where everyone was, he found everyone lying on the ground under the shade like dead bodies waiting to be decomposed into the soil.

"Did you find any water James??" asked George

On hearing this, Romilda and Andrew sat up hoping to receive some amount of water from James.

"No luck mate" replied James in a gloomy tone.

The three of them lay back as their hopes crashed into a hundred pieces.

"There are numerous amounts of rivers in the jungle; I don't know why we are not able to find one" said David

"I know that and I have been wondering the same since reaching into this part of the jungle" added in Andrew

"I don't think we will be able to find any water until we travel over somewhere far to get some" said David

"I think that the almighty has sucked all of the river from the earth and has only left a couple of drops for poor and innocent souls like us" moaned George who was fighting against the intense urge to drink water.

They kept feeding themselves with some wild berries and leftover fruits from the breakfast in order to help their throat with some amount of moisture.

However, the constant eating of the fruits had filled their tummies up and they could not force any more down their throats.

"Let's just rest for some time; if we have a good luck, then we might survive" said George

"No, I reckon we aren't getting any water if we don't make sincere efforts to search for it; it is not a living being that it will be able to walk and come to us" said David

"Yes, you are right David" added on Romilda while she continued to rest under the blissful shade of the tree

None of them except for Andrew and James got up.

"Guys, don't be lethargic, we will need to search for some water if we want some; get up and get to work" said David on seeing that Romilda and George still lying under the tree.

Romilda and George clumsily stood up and joined them.

"Good, now we split into two groups" said Andrew

"Romilda, George and David is one group and I will group along with James" "If anyone of us finds water, get your water bottles filled up and start looking for the other group"

After hearing to Andrew's instructions, they all dragged themselves into the quest for water and went into different directions.

In some time they were several hundred metres away from each other.

James and Andrew walked in all the moist areas to get traces of water and on the other hand Romilda, George and David randomly visited different spots to find some water.

They could neither find any traces of water nor could hear the noise of any streams. All they depended is their broken luck which was not cooperating with them at this point.

In a couple of minutes, they almost gave up until they found something unusual in the soil. James and Andrew noticed that the soil got wetter and wetter until it became completely liquified.

"There is liquid soil here; this is uncommon and there should be water here somewhere" said Andrew

"Yes, there must be a source of water which must be liquifying all this soil" added in James

Both of them used all their left-over energy to search in a radius of couple metres in the area.

They still were gravely disappointed as they failed to discover any water source.

On the other side George, Romilda and David had lost hope of discovering any water and proceeded back towards the place they were resting at.

James and Andrew began to proceed until James noticed something unusual in the ground.

He noticed the soil bubbled for a split second.

"Andrew did you see that??" asked James

"Saw what??"

"I think I just saw the liquified soil bubble up"

"No, that must be a mirage or an illusion of some sort; soil cannot bubble on its own, even if it is in liquid form" said Andrew

"What if the water is present around here but we are not checking the spots where it may be HIDDEN" said James in a unique and amplified tone

He walked towards the liquid soil pool and buried his hands into the soil. He lifted his hands up and threw away the soil accumulated on his hands.

He did this in a vigorous way until it proved to be extremely inefficient. He pulled out an empty bottle and let all the soil flow into it.

He threw the contents of the bottle until there was enough to give greater hints of water.

In some moments, the soil seemed to give out steam which burned his face.

In some moments, he was exposed to hot boiling water.

"Andrew! Here is the treasure but is it consumable??" asked James with enthusiasm

"James, you found water!!" "I will have to check whether it is consumable or not" said Andrew

Andrew bent down towards the source of hot water and let his hand slightly touch the surface of the boiling water. In some time, he sunk his entire palm into the water and pulled it out immediately. In some inspections, Andrew confirmed that it was drinkable water.

"This is drinkable water James!!! You are a genius" exclaimed Andrew

"Thanks a lot for the appreciation, Andrew but isn't this water too warm to be able to be consumed??" asked James

"Yes, but we can store it into our bottles and place it under the cool shade of the trees; will take some minutes to cool but the temperature will be optimum by then" said

Andrew

In some time they filled all of the bottles they had with the boiling water.

"Hey let's go and inform the other three about this; they must be dying from thirst" said James

"That is right" replied Andrew

They dashed back towards the place they came from where they found the three of them lying.

"We have found water!!" exclaimed James

They all were startled and stood up in fraction of a second.

"Are you kidding because I am really not in the mood to joke around" said George out of disbelief

" I am not kidding George; come with me and I will show you water" replied James

James and Andrew ran back towards the place they found water and David, Romilda and George followed them.

The three of them, who were unknown to water for quite a long time were having a roller coaster of emotions.

In a matter of seconds they had reached near the place they found the water.

"Where is the water??" asked George as his eyes magically looked for a river or a pond.

"Look down George" said James

George looked down to find a pool of water covered surrounded by soil.

"What, this is not consumable water!!" screamed George out of anger

"Yes, it is" said Andrew "I have checked it myself"

"Ok, so what are we waiting for; let's dive right in" said George

He bent over immediately and even before James could stop him, he had gulped down a bunch of water unknown of the fact that it was boiling hot. He spit the water out almost immediately and screamed in agony as he faced a robust burning sensation in his mouth.

"The water is boiling hot!!"

"Why didn't you inform me about this before I drank it" exclaimed George

"You did not give me any time to even stop you from doing so; you just went ahead and gulped down the water" said George

"How will we even drink the water if it is so hot??" asked Romilda

"Yes, we will have to cool it down in our water bottles; start filling them up" replied Andrew

They all began to fill up all the water bottles they had from the hot water mini pool.

The water level went down substantially as they filled up water in their bottles.

After they were done filling them up they went back to their rest place to get some shade for the bottles.

The water was so hot that their hands burned even if they held the bottle for some time.

They sat down immediately when they reached their rest place and instantaneously placed their water bottles under the shade of a tree onto a leaf to speed up the cooling down of the water.

Meanwhile, the water was cooling down, they waited in anticipation to get some water. George's thirst increased as he felt the burning sensation in his throat for some time and the boiling water left his throat drier than ever.

They waited for several minutes.

"I think that the water might be cool enough to be consumed by now" said Andrew

"Wait let me check" said James

James grasped a single bottle from a whole heap of them and uncapped it gently.

He let the water touch his lips barely until he felt pleasure of cool water and continued to gulp down the whole bottle.

The rest of them watched him in anticipation to get an answer from him.

"Is the water fine??" asked George

"Yes, it is great" replied James

On hearing this they were filled with pleasure and in some seconds everyone had caught on to a bottle for themselves.

They all drank the precious liquid until the powerful need of thirst drove away from their throats.

"The water feels so good" said George "Yes, it does; feels like we are drinking it after some several years" said Romilda agreeing to George.

After being finished with their respective portions of water, they went on to keep the empty bottles back.

"How did you find that water" asked David

"It was all James; he noticed that there was water in the ground and indeed there was water in there" said Andrew

"Thanks a lot James!!" exclaimed Romilda "Would have been dead soon if you would have not found any water

"Your welcome Romilda" "Andrew, we should not waste time and continue moving, but first of all let's fill some more water and hydrate ourselves completely" said James

"Yes, you are right; or else we will be lying dead around somewhere again"

They all finished the rest of the bottles to completely hydrate themselves until they could not drink anymore water.

They all went back and filled up the empty bottles of water they had and stuffed them into a single bag.

In some time they found themselves walking again.

"We need to be faster, or else there will be a high chance that we won't be able to reach Meraki today" said David

"I am going a bit faster so keep up with me" added on David

They continued to walk in a fast pace. They kept on keeping themselves fresh and energetic with water and fruits which they found on the way but were cautious enough to not drink a whole bunch of water in a single time.

The sky was clear and was partially blocked by the number of trees in the jungle. It stood clear and roared with wind. As it became windier and windier it became more and more difficult to continue to walk in the direction, opposite to the flow of the vigorous wind.

They had no choice except for continuing to walk in the same direction with all the strength they have to ensure they reach Meraki in time.

"Ouch!!" squeaked George

"What happened??" inquired James "Something hit my eye hard" replied George whilst pressed his fist against his left eye

"It feels like we are in a hurricane" cried out Romilda "It is so hard to carry on"

"Stop complaining people; in some time the wind shall stop" "Continue walking or else reaching Meraki will become a dream" said David

In some time the wind rested and turned into a lovely cold breeze which continued to help them stay fresh.

Out of the blue moon came out a single dart like stick which brushed past James' hands and struck a tree.

"What was that??" asked Andrew

"Whatever it was, I am lucky enough that it did not hit me" said James

"Yes, might be a broken sharp twig"

They continued assuming the dart thing was not a danger.

A strong gush of wind came nearby. All the bushes and trees vibrating vigorously.

Out of the blue moon, jumped out a huge stone like structure that leaped on James.

In some time James was beneath the creature struggling to escape its wreath.

The creature was colossal and its back was covered in sharp prickles.

All of them stared at it confused about how to help James.

Andrew rushed towards James and gave the creature a punch in its face to disrupt it from continuing to attack James.

It stepped back and Andrew took the opportunity to pull out James from the danger.

In a split second it regained its vision and locked its target on Andrew, running towards Andrew with a stunning speed it intended to hit him in the gut.

As he came by, Andrew stepped away to dodge the hit and to avoid the menace.

The creature crashed into the tree.

David gathered courage and hit it with a wooden log which lay lifeless near him.

The creature, with full of confusion chased David. David ran for his life. Andrew ran towards David to help him.

Meanwhile James, found Andrew's bag around him and picked it up immediately. Skimming through the glass vials, he managed to locate a familiar one. He tore apart a small piece of his cloth and applied the liquid from the vial on the cloth.

He dashed in the direction with Andrew's bag hanging on his shoulder and a piece of cloth in his hands towards David.

As he spotted the creature, he instantaneously picked up a stone and chucked it towards the peace disruptor.

The stone hit it in the eye burring out its vision.

James dashed towards it and agitated it further by chucking another stone at it.

Meanwhile Romilda and George were busy hiding behind the tee to avoid the danger.

The creature ran with all the speed towards James intending to kill it. James jumped over it but came in contact with its back causing him to bleed.

The creature leaped again on James.

James quickly pulled out the cloth and forced it against its nose.

Soon the creature calmed down eventually falling unconscious.

"Are you fine kid??" inquired Andrew as he helped James to get up.

"What in the world was that??" asked George from a distance

"That is a piranota" replied Andrew

"Yes, those are extremely dangerous and can suck your soul out of your body in seconds." Added in David

Andrew noticed blood dripping from James' arms.

"How did this happen to you??" asked Andrew

"As I jumped over this thing, some of the prickles came in contact with my hand"

"Oh boy!! You are the one who puts yourself in danger to save us always" said Andrew

"You almost took the soul out of my body when you were fighting against the piranota"

"How did you manage to make it unconscious??" asked David

"I found Andrew's bag lying beside me when someone distracted the animal" "I searched the bag and found the liquid that you used to make George unconscious; that is how I managed to fight it" replied James

"Ahh, that was a cheeky move, well done; but let's get away from here as soon as possible" "We never know whether the effects of the liquid will last forever" said David

"James, your wound is deep, we will need to stop the blood flowing out of your body" said Andrew

He reached out his hand into his bag and pulled out a piece of cloth. He tied it tightly around James' wounded arm and applied a potion to replenish his skin back faster.

"Thanks Andrew"

They started walking after James' arm was all set.

In some time they reached far beyond the life threatening piranota's reach.

They had walked by several hundred metres in a couple of minutes to completely avoid the danger of any further creatures of the jungle.

In some time they approached river which was leading to a high waterfall.

The river ran into the waterfall. They filled up their bottles of water again with fresh river water and soon ran into a waterfall.

They were filled with confusion on what to do next.

"Hey where do we walk next David" asked Andrew

"I don't know; the map shows that you walk further straight but there is a waterfall in front of us" replied David

"I think then we will have to pave our way through the waterfall and jump down into the river" said George attempting to crack a joke

"That is not funny George; we are stuck in a completely peculiar situation and you are cracking jokes which aren't even funny" said Romilda

"I reckon George wasn't joking" said Andrew as he looked into the map

"What do you mean??" asked James

"It means that we will have to go through the waterfall to continue"

"Wait, there is no way to even do that" "Isn't there any other way??"

"There is another way; we can take the route that we were taking the previous time but for that we will have to walk back some several miles and we won't be reaching Meraki until tomorrow"

"That is not even an option" said James

"I think that we will have to take the risk and jump into the river"

"No James!! That is far too hazardous"

"We don't have any other option and it is not that the water is going to hurt us bad"

"You just need to jump into the river" said James

"I don't even know how to swim; I will be screwed up if I jump into this berserk river"

"Ok, so you can jump in the after everyone has done it; by then there will be plenty of people to help you down there" replied James

"Sounds like we have a plan" added in Andrew

"We will have to do this, we don't even have an option"

"Ok, but I will go in the end" said George

"Yes, first up will be David, then me, then James Romilda and George in the end" said Andrew

"Ok, fine with us"

"I reckon that someone should go after George" said James

"And why do you think that??" asked Andrew

"George will be too scared to even jump from up here; If we all will be up here, then there will be no one there to ensure that he jumps" said James

"Thanks, James for boosting my confidence on another level" said George in a sarcastic tone

"That is right James; David I think then you should be the one who should be going last, George will be second last"

"No problem" replied David

"Ok, so who is the first one up??" asked James

"That would be me" replied Andrew in a serious tone sounding scared from the height he was standing at.

He stepped forward towards the end of the cliff took some deep breathes to release some of the terror and anxiety away from himself.

He grasped onto his bag tighter and leaped into the splashing river.

In some time he went with the fast flow of the river and did not seem to stop.

Andrew tried to hold onto the river bank but the rapid flow of the rover prevented him to grasp onto anything to stop him. In a matter of seconds, he was flowing away from the river.

"Andrew is not stopping!!" screamed Romilda

"We will have to jump" said James

"You right" added in George

"No, everyone at once" "Everyone hold hands and jump into the river on the count of three"

"1...2...3!!" screamed James as everyone jumped high up into the river.

All of them landed into the river at the same time, creating a huge splash. With them covered in water and into the extreme river; their vision was blurred out. They tried to grab onto something themselves but instead held onto some loose twigs not allowing them to stop themselves from flowing away.

Water filled into them as they all drenched into the pool of rapidly flowing fear and anxiety.

In some time they could see specks of water droplets in the sky.

The rapid flow of water did not allow them grasp onto anything and in some time their eyelids closed gradually.

They were pulled out from their conscious and pushed into unconsciousness.

As the waves from the river lashed against each other, they stayed afloat unconscious on the surface of river flowing with the river in a rapid pace.

The pace of the river stayed constant and so did their movement into the river.

In some time a noise could be heard from somewhere nearby as the feeling of nausea was interrupted.

"James, James" said Andrew as he woke James up.

He shook James vigorously but James did not seem to respond. He pressed against his stomach to remove the amount of water gathered in him.

Then he went onto pressing his hands against his chest firmly to startle up James and waking him up eventually.

James gradually opened his eyes and gave a quick before sitting upright.

He coughed for some time because of the cold water inside him. The feeling of nausea was still erect inside him.

He saw Andrew, flooding his mind with millions of questions.

"Andrew, is it you" asked James to verify that he was not dreaming

"Yes, it is Andrew" replied Andrew

He helped James to come back on his feet.

James' bag was still hanging on his back, seemingly stuck to it.

James looked around to see people walking around him. Several people buzzed around from one shop to another.

Some distinct kinds of creatures which were mounted by people were also visible.

He could see numerous huts into the area with a pungent smell of blossoms. In some distance he could see a garden behind which lay a majestical castle with colossal walls and millions of variant colours of flowers surrounding its walls.

The sky was pinkish-orange in colour and revealed the sun and the moon in far distance together at the same time.

James could not believe his eyes and contemplated his life. He thought he was living a dream which soon transformed into a reality.

"Andrew, where are we?? And how did we reach here" asked James

"We are in Meraki" replied Andrew

"What, how come did we reach here??" "I know that you were in the river and then all of us also jumped in"

"And where are George, Romilda and David??"

"I will answer all your questions; right now, just come with me" said Andrew

Andrew started to walk as James followed him blankly.

They stopped in front of a board with a handprint on it.

"Why did we stop here??" asked James

"Because we have reached where we needed to" replied back Andrew

Before James could further interrogate him, Andrew put out his hand on the board.

"Step back James" said Andrew

James and Andrew stepped back towards as they both could hear and feel some vibrations from the ground.

In some seconds a chamber popped out of the ground. James kept gazing as it going towards the top.

"Step into the chamber"

They both stepped in and soon they were descending into the ground.

All that was visible to them was darkness. In some time, they had reached down a mysterious hall. There lay a table around which George, Romilda and David were sitting around.

As they saw James, they dashed towards James.

Romilda threw her arms around James hugging him tightly.

"I thought that you were dead" said Romilda

"Well I am not" said James as they all giggled on it for some time.

"I am still confused though; how come did we end up here, in Meraki through the river" "I thought that it was the last time my eyes were open" said James

"That river came into Meraki; we had been floating in it for hours" "The people in Meraki saw us and helped us out of the river" said Andrew

"Might have been a rough ride for all of you" said James

"Not really for us, only for you" said Andrew

"What do you mean??"

"Supposedly you were on the verge of sinking when you were found in the river. We had to get a person jump into the river to get you out of its wrath"

"Ohh, I might have been lucky enough to survive"

"Well you were" said David

"Now let's stop talking and do some eating" said George "I am sure that James might be starving after all he hasn't had a bite since hours"

"Yes I am starving"

They all took a seat around the table. Andrew clapped his hands twice, until some people showed up with numerous amounts of plates stacked up on their hands.

The all carefully placed the plates on the table.

The plates were filled with food of different kinds.

In a matter of seconds they started munching on everything in front of them.

"Finally some good food!!" moaned George as he ate the delicious steak

"Yes, I had been tired of eating fruits and vegetables; felt like I am a cow " said Romilda

"Romilda, cows don't eat fruits and vegetables; they eat grass" said George

"You know what I mean and so do I" "Don't contemplate about what I say; process my feelings and you will understand me better"

"Ok, Ok no need to become a philosopher"

They stuffed their mouths with whatever they could land their hands on next as the hunger for good food had gathered in their minds and stomachs.

In some time they were done with their delicious meal.

"Andrew, now that we have found James and have also had our dinner, I think that it is time for us to get back to work" said Romilda

"What work??" asked Andrew

"The work for which we came here!! Returning back to Earth"

"Oh yes, that slipped out of my mind" "It is already dark outside; people might be resting at this hour" "I reckon that we should also take some rest and think about how to get you back tomorrow"

"I don't have any problem with that" said Romilda

"Andrew, a quick question; what was that castle??" asked James

"Ohh, it is the place where the people in Archade hold meetings occasionally" "There might be some people residing there, but I don't live there"

"That is a pretty amazing castle from the outer looks of it" added in George

"Yes, that has been made by more than a 1000 extremely talented workers"

"Took quite some time to build that thing up"

"I figured that out as soon as I saw it"

"Yes, I think that you must slide in some rest for yourself now" said Andrew

"Yes, time for you people to go to bed; next morning isn't going to be a smooth one" said David

In some time they were leaded out from the dining hall and into the bedroom, through the corridors.

The bedroom was covered with artifacts and crafts of the native people of Meraki. The bedroom had just enough beds for all of them to sleep.

"Here are your beds; make yourself comfortable; we will be meeting tomorrow in the morning next" said Andrew as he and David walked out of the bedroom proceeding to their own room

"This place is so cool; I presumed that Meraki might be proper village with only huts" said George

"Seems like your judgement has been proven wrong" said James

James, Romilda and George walked around the room exploring it little by little. They admired the intricate paintings in the room near their beds and the Arti crafts that hung on the walls increasing the beauty of the blank wall behind it.

In some time the lights went off automatically and the door of the bedroom opened by itself.

"Who is it??" screamed out James

"It is me James" said Andrew

"Andrew, what in the world are you doing??"

"Reminding you to go to bed" replied Andrew

"Ok, ok we will be sleeping soon but at least turn the lights back on"

"I won't; I want to make sure that you people sleep properly; your bodies have been through a lot of pain and you need to give it some rest"

"Now get into your bed"

"Andrew, my clothes are filthy, do you have some other clothes for us??"

Andrew turned the lights back on. He walked into the corridor and came back with a stack of vibrant and distinct coloured clothes.

"Here are some; you three select your clothes and wear them"

"I am trusting you with the sleeping thing" said Andrew as he left the pile of clothes into the room and left

James, Romilda and George were pleased to get out of their old and filthy clothes covered in mud and dirt from top to bottom. They quickly wore some new jumpers and climbed into their beds before Andrew could come back again.

"How do you switch the lights off??" asked James

"Andrew told that as soon as all the beds are filled up, they turn off automatically"

Before George could finish with his sentence the lights in the room went off and they were left with deafening silence in the room.

"There you go; now let's sleep" said James as all of them abandoned their stressful thoughts and began to enjoy the sleep they were about to receive

After they got some hours of comfortable and relaxing sleep they opened their eyes. James, Romilda and George got ready within an hour and found Andrew waiting for them outside their room already.

"So how was the sleep guys??" asked Andrew

"It was more than mesmerising; my back hadn't touched anything soft as the bed till yesterday night" said George

"Yes, it was amazing to have an actual bed to sleep on" added on James

"Good, you guys enjoyed the sleep"

"Now let's go and have breakfast" said Andrew as he lead them into the dining hall

They had their breakfast in a couple of minutes

"So what next Andrew??" asked Romilda

"Now we go to the castle" replied Andrew

"In some time I and David have a meeting regarding you people which is organized by me"

"Come on now, follow me, not a lot of walking to do today"

The five of them walked out of the cabinet which brought them down to Andrew's place. They were exposed to a handful of pleasurable sunlight dancing around the village of Meraki.

Everyone was in the market; buying stuff and some riding carts.

They watched the marvel of Meraki as they walked towards the extreme lovely castle surrounded by a circular garden of flowers.

As they closed in, gates of the castle opened. In some time, they were into the colossal walls of the castle which had several designs engraved into its walls.

There were several rooms with authorized people going into and coming out of it.

Hundreds of people fluttered past the five of them as they walked for some seconds deep into the castle.

At last they arrived by a wooden board and the words "Conference room" were engraved in bold on it.

"We have reached the conference room" "Come on in" said Andrew

"What?? We will also have to come into the conference room, we thought that only you and David will be going in" said Romilda

"Seems like you have to come into the conference room; they might want to know the situation you three are caught up in by you only"

"Now let's not waste time and go in; don't be afraid, they will ask you questions but very basic ones"

As they all stepped into the room, they could see a some couplets of shelves full of documents lined up behind the table in front of them. The table was circular in shape and was surrounded by chairs with people already sitting on them.

There was a vintage clock hanging on the wall lifelessly. They were told by Andrew to grab any chair and have a seat.

As they all sat down and took a good two minutes to settled down, the meeting commenced.

"I may start the meeting now if everyone is ready" said Andrew

Everyone gave a slight nod.

"Ok, first of all I sincerely thank all of you present here to come for a meeting on such a short notice"

"The motion of the meeting might be clear to all of you; it is basically about the return of these three children to their world"

"This is George, Romilda and James" said Andrew as he introduced all of them

"They will require the help of you, the extremely experienced people of this council to make a successful return"

"Now gentlemen, if you may want to ask any questions to them, you may go ahead" said Andrew as he sat back on his chair

There was a deafening silence in the room as Andrew completed with his sentence.

Sometime later a voice was raised by an elderly man with a long white beard and curly hair. He seemed old by his looks and carried an intense look on his face which intimated Romilda, James and George.

"I would like to ask them something with your permission Andrew"

"Go ahead"

"Before discussing the solution of the problem, we will need absolutely all the details that you have about the incident"

"And before going into the depth of it, please inform about HOW did you arrive here, into our world??"

As the old man, completed with his question he sat back on his seat expecting an answer from either three of them.

The three of them were in sheer shock and looked at each other blankly without anyone of them standing up to answer the question.

"Anyone from you three can answer his question; please do not consume so much time of the committee meeting" said Andrew breaking the silence of the room.

After the interruption by Andrew, James stood to answer the question.

"The transfer of us to this world happened because of a prophecy that just sucked us in into it and the next thing we found were we were stranded in the middle of nowhere" said James

"Where did you find this prophecy and how did it look like??"

"We found it in our school restricted room and it looked like a crystal clear normal prophecy" replied James

"Ok, That is it from our side"

James sat down as his anxiety rested.

"Does anyone else have any questions??" asked Andrew

A hand was raised in the air by a somewhat young contender of the council.

"Yes, you may go ahead" said Andrew

"Since how long have you three been here??"

This time Romilda stood up to answer the question

"We haven't kept a count but has been quite some days since we have been here"

"Where did you find Andrew?"

"We found him injured in the midst of the jungle" replied Romilda to another person who raised a question The meeting continued until everyone received the piece of information they required and were soon tired of shooting questions at James, Romilda and George.

"Ok, does anyone else have any question" said Andrew There was a long pause.

"I consider that as a no; James, Romilda and George may leave the office room and go to their respective place" "David will lead you there" said Andrew

In some time, the three of them were taken back to Andrew's place by David.

"Why did they kick us out of the conference room and they still stayed in??" asked George as they walked towards Andrew's place

"There is some information that they decide on to whether they must give you or not; I myself find myself having a lack of information" "There are some matters about which they cannot tell you about" said David

"But how would it harm them if we know about the stuff they know; nothing like we are imposters and have come to raid this village" said Romilda

"I don't have all the answers to your questions; ask them to Andrew" "I am just doing what they are asking me to; at the end of the day I need to make a living" said David

In some time they had reached the dark residing of Andrew

"Here you go, I have some work; I am going out but don't go anywhere outside until Andrew comes" said David as he left the place.

"What will we even do??" asked George

"There is nothing we can do other than wait for Andrew to come" said James

"No, I am telling that what shall we do until he comes, I am getting bored"

"Maybe you can go back to sleep again" said Romilda

"I already have slept for like 10 hours; I don't feel like sleeping at all"

"Do whatever you want to but don't annoy us"

"What do you think, will we be able to go back to our homes??" asked James

"I don't have any idea; I don't have any regrets coming here though" replied George

"Yes, this place is great but I do want to go back home" said Romilda

"The council was so intimidating; especially the person who was asking a bunch of questions in such a serious tone" said George

"Yes, I got pretty scared by them for a moment" added in James

"By when will Andrew be back??" asked Romilda

"David said that he would be back in some time" replied George

Soon, it was post lunch time. They could hear the lift descending into the chamber knowing that Andrew had arrived.

They woke up from their inconsistent sleep and went forward to meet Andrew.

When they saw him, he was covered in sweat and his clothes were covered in mud

"Where had you been Andrew and what has happened to your clothes??" asked Romilda

"I have been here and there after the meeting ended, nothing to worry about" replied Andrew as he set his bag down on the doorstep

"George can you grab some water for me??"

"Sure"

George went back into the kitchen to grab some water for Andrew who was drenched in sweat.

They sat down to have a quick snack.

"Nice food, I must say" said Andrew

Andrew carried a tensed look on his face.

In some time James noticed it.

"Andrew what happened in the conference??" asked James trying to get to know what had happened

"You mean the council right"

"Yes, the council" "Nothing, just talked about how to get you out of this situation" said Andrew

"Why are you acting weird Andrew" asked James

"Is something wrong??"

"No, James you are just imagining things"

"Ohh, then why am I seeing this tensed look on your face??"

"Ok, Ok, I cannot handle it in anymore"

"I am telling you guys but don't tell that I told you this to anyone, not even to David"

"Tell what??" asked George

The three of them carefully listened to Andrew as he started talking

"Today, in the council meeting, we figured that getting you all back would be next to impossible" said Andrew

"Wait what!!" screamed Romilda

"Listen carefully" "There was this another prophecy which is already long lost which is supposed to be connected to the prophecy in your world" said Andrew

"But no one knows where it is and supposedly it is the only way to get you people back" said Andrew

"So you think that there is no way that we are getting back to Earth" said George

"No, it is not impossible; you will have to find the prophecy and there is a strong chance that you will get back safely"

"Does anyone have any idea about where it is??" asked James

"No, if they would have had some idea about the whereabouts of the prophecy, then I would have known about it" replied Andrew

After Andrew's disappointing words the room was filled silence. Everyone took some moments to contemplate about their situation whilst Andrew was waiting for anyone of them to speak up.

"Can anyone speak something??" asked Andrew as his patience level had been surpassed

"Yes, Yes, I think that I am angry" whispered Romilda

"Angry??" asked Andrew

"Yes, had it not been for your stupid room, we would not have ended up here James!!" screamed Romilda as she stood up

"Calm down Romilda!!" said George

"What are you talking about Romilda; it has been a long time since that has happened, what is the point of bringing it up right now" said James trying to defend himself

"You should have not brought up going into that terrible room and we would have been fine"

"We are stuck here now, maybe even forever"

"Romilda, this is not an extremely bad place after all to stay at" said George trying to make Romilda feel better

"George, nice try but you are not helping here" said James

"I don't know about anything; James you got us into this mess and you will have to get us out of this too" said Romilda as she stood up and dashed into the room

"Romilda, wait!!" said George

"Leave her alone for some time George" said Andrew

"Don't worry James, she is just frustrated; don't take anything she said seriously"

"No Andrew, she was not wrong" "This is all my fault and I have to do something to get us out of here and you are the person who will be helping me"

"Don't act foolish James, it has been barely 24 hours of you being in Meraki and you don't even know anything about this place"

"Don't even try going out searching for the prophecy by yourself; it is still a dangerous job" said Andrew attempting to stop James from what he was thinking.

"I will need to go now; I have some work in another council" "This is my advice; don't do anything that will hurt you or your friends" said Andrew as he left

"Thanks Andrew" replied James

George and James went into the room where they found Romilda buried inside her bed.

"Hey, why are you acting weird??" asked James

Romilda pulled the sheets down revealing her intensely irritated and frustrated face.

"I am not acting weird James, I am scared" "I don't want to live away from the place where I originate from"

"I do not care how good this place is; I just want to go back" said Romilda as a tear rolled down her cheek

"I will look at it for sure; I promise you that in some time we will be good and soon be back" said James as he left the room

George followed James outside in the corridor confused and concerned from James' words to Romilda

"What were you thinking when you said that to Romilda?" said George

"What are you talking about"

"Didn't Andrew make himself clear enough??" "And how will you even figure this out if even Andrew and his fellow council colleagues can't find a way out?" said George

"I guess we will have to do some of the brainstorming of ours" replied James

"Don't do anything foolish James like you did in the school"

"We have faced enough trouble in the last few days; I don't think that our mind is ready for anymore"

"I will take care of that mate" "I think it is snack time, I am starving; let's go and grab a bite" said James diverting the flow of the conversation into another way.

While the both of them ate, James had sunk into the deep thoughts about the prophecy. His anxiety rose has he pondered more over the topic.

By the time they were finished with their snacks, the sun had set down and it was quite dark outside. Some hints of light could be seen through the sky but the rest was covered by a dark and colourless mask.

In some time David came back into the place.

"So how is everyone??" asked David

"Everything is somewhat fine" replied George

"Somewhat??"

"Yes, Romilda and James had a small fight but that is fine, they have forgotten about it"

"Ok, I reckon there is nothing to worry about so will leave the matter to you"

"By the way, there might have been some progress for your case" said David

"Wait really!!" squeaked George

"Yes, I will tell you about it at dinner in detail while Andrew is present so I don't pass on some false information of my own"

"I might be resting in my room; come in whenever if you require something" said David as he walked into his room

"Sure will keep that in mind"

George walked back into the room finding James and Romilda fast asleep. George could not do anything so forced himself to some sleep too. In a couple of hours, they woke up from their clumsy subconscious as the dinner time came on its way in.

Andrew had been there in the room, waking up everyone from their sleep.

"I see, you guys caught some sleep" said Andrew

"Yes, the beds are too comfortable to keep us away" said George

"Ok, but it is dark outside; get up it is time for dinner" said Andrew

"Coming in some time"

"Hey James, I am sorry for the way I screamed at you" said Romilda out of nowhere

"It is fine Romilda; I did not mind you screaming on me" replied James

"Yes, please forget about everything I said"

"Hey, you both talk about this later; we need to go outside now" "Andrew will flip out if we don't go outside in some time" said George

In some time they found themselves eating dinner outside.

As they ate dinner George remembered about the good news David was talking about.

"Hey David, remember you said that there is some progress in our case in the council" "What was that about??"

"Oh yes, I think that Andrew can answer that better than me" said David

"What are you both talking about??" asked Andrew in confusion

On hearing this George gave David an extremely weird look.

"Remember what the elder most person said in the council Andrew"

"Yes, yes, a person in our council does believe that there is surely a way that we can go back"

"That is good right" said James

"Not quite a good news because the person has been acting crazy since some time according to other people in the council" "Some of my sources said that he has been crying over his wife's death but she had died some time ago" "He also mixed rum with milk and drank it in the council saying that it tasted good" "After that he insisted us on trying the same" "Might just say that that was the most hilarious thing that everyone had seen in the council" said Andrew

"So why is this person even in the council??" asked Romilda

"I thought about it too but supposedly he comes out to be the oldest person in whole of the Meraki and knows most about it and its secret hideouts" said Andrew

"We don't treasure him but the knowledge"

"We have been trying to squeeze most of the information that he beholds but he doesn't give it away as easily"

"It is not a news to be celebrate upon; just a slight spark on the matter today in the council" said Andrew

"There might be something be something he knows but none of you know about" said James

"You must utilize him usefully"

"We figured that soon enough James" said Andrew

In some time they were finished with their dinner and were fast asleep again.

The rest morning was an unusual one.

With everyone concealed inside their homes, they could find no one outside wondering around in the miraculous grounds of Meraki

"There is no one outside" said James as he came back from outside

"There might be some sort of weather uncertainty in the village so people might be preferring to stay inside" said George

"How can they even predict the weather in Meraki??" asked Romilda

"I don't know; let's go question Andrew about this" said George

The three of them went down to Andrew's room finding him sleep till now.

"I reckon we should not be disturbing him; he has a lot to deal with right now" "Let him rest" said Romilda

"You are right and we also have the option of asking David" said James

The three of them dashed into David's room finding him asleep too.

"Why are both of them sleeping till now" "It has been quite late; they should be up by now" said George

"Let's not disturb them now; we can ask them when they wake up"

James, Romilda and George went back into their room contemplating about the growing laziness of Andrew and David.

The simply sat back in their room waiting eagerly for Andrew and David to wake up from their deep sleep.

As some time passed by they could hear the door slamming in some distance.

They found Andrew in his night suite in the corridor.

"Hey, why were you and David sleeping for so long??" asked Romilda

"Yes, and we went outside to catch some fresh air but found no one outside" "Felt like this was an abandoned village" said George

"Ohh, did I not tell you about the holiday in Meraki??" asked Andrew

"No, we certainly don't remember you saying this" said James

"Might have slipped out of my mind, today is like the holiday throughout Meraki" "No one goes to work today and this day comes once every month" "It seems like that people just enjoy being in the comfort of their homes and avoid going outside on this day" said Andrew

"Nice, seems like a good holiday in Meraki"

"Anyways, if you want anything we will be right by the hall" said Romilda as they walked into the hall

"This is so cool" said George

"These people have more chill Sundays than us"

"Yes, but only once a month"

Meanwhile James was pondering about something totally different Romilda and George were busy discussing about something else.

James ran into David's room and gave him a few vigorous shakes to wake him up from his sleep.

"Hey, wake up David" said James

"I am already awake; what do you need James??" asked David

"Can you tell me the person who was telling that he knew something about the prophecy in the council"

"And why would you want to know that??" asked David

"Just something came across my mind" "Mostly want to know the people in the council" said James

"His name would be Henry muller"

"Where might he be living?"

"I think he might be living right by the castle; there might be a board of his name on his house too saying that he is a lunatic which interestingly enough was pinned by him"

"Ok, that is what I needed back from you; you might want to go back to your sleep" "Sorry for disturbing you" said James as he walked out of the room.

David drifted back to his deep sleep while James went out with the name Henry muller in his head.

James walked out through the hall and went towards the lift which lead the way out.

"Where are you going??" asked George

"Nowhere, just going out to get some fresh air; you guys carry on" replied James

"Do you want us to join you??"

"No, I wish for some alone time; you know just getting my mind cleared"

James walked away on saying this and soon found himself in the grounds of the market with everything shut proceeding towards the castle.

The market seemed awkward as it did not rumble a tumble like usual.

In some time James reached by the castle, frantically looking for Henry's house.

Right by the castle were the flowers and that was all that he could see.

He went to the other side to find himself in front of a wooden board with the words "House of a lunatic" engraved on it in bold letters.

He figure that it was the way to Henry's home.

He walked in towards the board and found something written in minute letters. "The people move forward and so do you to find the residing of Henry" was written on it as James had a closer look.

He followed what the board said and found himself in front of a colossal wooden infrastructure with lamps hanging all over it.

The entrance was weirdly surrounded by creepy skulls of dead people and as James walked through the entrance where he found the door to enter the house.

He knocked on the door twice. He waited until no one answered. As James was about to leave the scary premised of Henry; he heard a noise from the inside.

"Come in" said the person as it rang inside James' head.

He reached back over to the door and gave it a gentle push and found it open.

The door gave a creaking noise as it gently pushed against the dusty surface of the floor.

James made his way in to find a huge hall with a chair tilted the other way around.

The whole room was messed up and everything seemed upside down.

Out of nowhere, came out an old person with a long beard and was almost bald.

He wore a dirty cloak with eaten up eggs and bacon dragged all over it.

"Who are you??" asked James

"I am the great Henry muller"

"What do you need from me my friend??" asked Henry

"Nothing, I figured that you know my friends Andrew and David"

"Yes, I do, they are in the Archade"

"Yes, I have come to discuss about something related to it"

"Go ahead kid, tell me whatever you want to; I am an open book"

James found the way Henry spoke extremely unusual.

James froze for a moment until there was an interruption from Henry.

"My friend, you wanted to tell me something right" said Henry

"Yes, Yes, Sorry I got lost" "I heard from Andrew that you had something related to us returning back to Earth.

"Are you one from the three people who have come from some other world??" asked Henry

"Yes, I am James" spoke out James nervously

"Ohh, I feel unfortunate for you three; we are trying to figure out to get you back" said Henry

"Thank you sir but I needed the information you had about the prophecy" said James

"I do not have any information; I don't have anything on that" said Henry hesitantly

James could notice the change in tone and behaviour of Henry and figured that he was hesitating on answering his question.

"But you said that you had something on getting us back" said James

"Yes, I did but that does not mean that I have the where abouts of the prophecy"

"I never asked about the whereabouts of the prophecy"

"I figured that you would soon so I brought it out before you asked for it so that we could save each other's time"

"Sir, are you fine??" asked James

"I have never been better" said Henry in an unusual manner

"That good friend of yours is Andrew right" said Henry

"Yes, he is; he is the one who helped us to come here"

"Yes, extremely talented young man; he is of utmost importance in our council"

"Yes, I got to know about it recently too"

"Nice, Nice; would you like some rum with milk??" asked Henry handing over a huge glass to James

"I am good sir" replied James as he placed the glass down

"You should try rum with milk; not a bad combination after all"

"Sure, I am just not in the mood for It today"

"Ok, Ok, you can try it later whenever you want to"

"I reckon I might have to go somewhere; Andrew had called me at this time" said James as he looked at the time.

"Sure, who am I to stop you??"

James soon went out of the house as Henry bid him goodbye

James walked back contemplating about the peculiar behaviour that Henry showed.

He ran back into Andrew's place as it had been dark outside and cold too.

"Where had you been??" asked Romilda

"Yes, we were actually worried about you" added on George

"I was just wondering outside in the village by myself" "I was enjoying a bit too much outside so I did not keep a track of time" said James

"Anyways, we have to have dinner; come on in" said Romilda as she pulled James in for dinner

As they walked in the dining area, he found David and Andrew sitting there waiting for the three of them

"I am not that hungry" said James

"What?? You will have to eat something James" "You are a growing boy"

"No, Andrew, I had a heavy snack" "I am fine"

"As you wish James, but if you want something, it is right by here"

"Sure, thanks for telling" said James as he dashed into his room and lay on his bed directly

In some time George and Romilda came into the room finding him on his bed contemplating about something deeply whilst he lay on his bed.

"Hey mate" said George. James did not reply to George.

Romilda and James walked towards James and gave him some shakes.

James was startled and sat upright on his bed.

"What is up with you James??" asked Romilda

"Nothing"

"No, there is something fishy; you did not even have dinner; you were wandering in the open for so long and now you were thinking about something that you will not tell us about" said George

"Ok, I need to tell you something about today which I found quite peculiar"

"I will tell you in some time after Andrew and David go into their rooms" said James

Sometime later Andrew came in to wish them good night. Switching the lights off he went back this room.

James creeped out of the room opening the door extremely gently.

He chased Andrew outside in the corridor. James saw Andrew's light go out in some time and dashed back in the room.

"Where did you go??" asked Romilda

"To make sure that Andrew had fallen asleep" replied James

"Ok what was the thing you were going to tell us about??" asked George

"Yes, so today I did not go out for fresh air and to roam around in the open" "I lied to you people"

"But why??" inquired Romilda "Yes, and where did you go??" asked George

"I had gone to Henry's house" said James

"Who in the world is Henry now??" asked George

"The person who was showing some positive signs about our return and the person who David was talking about" replied James

"How did you get his name and address??" asked George

"I took advantage of David being in deep sleep today late morning"

"But why did you have to go there??" asked Romilda

"Of, course to discuss about the prophecy" said James

"Ohh, so did you get any information on that topic??"

"No, unfortunately I did not; I wanted to talk about this only" "When I asked him about the prophecy, he started acting extremely peculiarly and was hesitating to answer my question"

"He kept changing the topic and offered me some rum with milk"

"What you drank rum with milk??" asked George

"No of course I did not drink rum with milk!!" "He only offered it to me; did not force it down my throat"

"Not going to lie but if that drink would have gone down my throat, I would have been dead at that very moment" said James

"Let's talk about the rum later" "Coming to the prophecy, if he would be hesitating so much; then there is definitely something which he knows and we don't know about" said Romilda

"Yes, I figured that I do think that if we squeeze some of the information out of him; it might help us a whole ton to get back" said James

"No doubt in that; but the question is how"

"I think that that is something we will need to figure out" said George

"Do we tell about this to Andrew though??" asked James

"No! not right now" replied Romilda

"Tell me what??" came voice from some distance.

In some seconds, the lights of their room turned on and they found Andrew standing right by the door.

"Andrew, what are you doing here; didn't you go to sleep" said Romilda

"I did but thirst is something I can't stand so I was just going to get some water" "When I walked past this room I could hear you outside; I reckon you were talking about something about telling me something"

"What would that be now??" inquired Andrew

"I think that you did not hear us properly" said James

"We were just not that sleepy so we were talking about something"

"And what would that something be??"

"Nothing, just football" said George hesitantly

"Yes, Yes, we were talking about football" added in James

"What is football??" asked Andrew in confusion

"Football is the most famous sport in our world" said George

"Ohh, that is something beyond my expertise" "You guys continue but ensure that you get some sleep in too" said Andrew as he went out of the room switching the lights off and shutting the door close.

"We would have been screwed right here" said Romilda

"I think that we should discuss about this tomorrow morning" said Romilda

"Yes, you are absolutely right, Andrew might here us again if we keep talking now" whispered James

On saying this everyone went to a deep sleep.

"Come on wake up people" said Andrew as he came in to wake up James, George and Romilda

"It is another new day; a lot of work to be done with" said Andrew

"We have another council meeting today"

"Do we need to come there??" asked George

"No, you don't need to be there and you aren't allowed too" "Not my decision, the council's decision" said Andrew trying to clarify himself

"Come on Andrew, we are already late" called out David

"Coming!!" "You guys, get ready and have your breakfast" "We will be gone for a good 3 to 4 hours" said Andrew

"It is becoming boring to stay indoors and sit idle all the time Andrew"

"Anything you have for us to do??" asked George

"No, and I am late for the council meeting so I will need to run quickly" said Andrew as he rushed out of the room

"What will we do now?" asked George

"Nothing, just do what Andrew said; eat your breakfast and I guess chill" said James

"Didn't we need to talk about something??" asked Romilda

"Yes, we do" replied James "But in some time" added in George

"First let's enjoy our breakfast and then we can worry about this"

"Ok, come on, the breakfast would be ready already" said James

Some minutes later they were seated back in their room, after having their breakfast.

"Must say today's breakfast was amazing" said George

"Yes, the bacon was especially delicious" added in James

"And the eggs were a delicacy"

"Now can we just stop discussing about this and talk about what we have to" said Romilda trying to interrupt their flow of conversation

"Ok! Fine" sighed George

"Yes so what do we do about it??" asked Romilda

"About what??" asked George

"About Henry" replied Romilda

"What can we possibly do anything unless we take some help from Andrew" said James

"I don't think that we should take Andrew's help so soon because I believe that he might tell us to stop"

"Yes, I agree; I reckon we will need to crack some idea to get some info from Henry ourselves" said James

"And if we are successful we can inform about it to Andrew later" "After all he also needs some of the precious information for the betterment of the village" added in Romilda

"Yes agreed"

"I think that I have an idea" said George

"What??" asked Romilda "Why don't we go to his house but this time, with more people to pressure him and with some luck in hand, we might be able to crack him open"

"Not a bad idea George!!" said James "Yes, I am quite surprised that you managed to get a decent idea up your sleeve given that you are so dumb" said Romilda

"I must say that you are not an encouraging person Romilda" said George

"I was just joking"

"So when do we go?" asked James

"We can go right now" said Romilda

"Right now!!" "Yes, why not" "Isn't it too early right now??" asked George

"If we delay going there any further, we might not be able to come back before Andrew and David" said Romilda

"They will be back in some hours and if we wait more, we won't be able to go out without them knowing"

"Sounds right, let's go right now then" said James

"Ok, I have no problem" added in George

The three of them went outside. James led them to Henry's house.

"What is this board??" asked George

"This board shows the way to Henry's house" replied James

"I know that but why does it say house of a lunatic on it??"

"Interestingly, David told me that he is a crazy person and has pinned this board by himself"

"I am getting scared now" "He won't harm us or anything right James"

"No, No, he is just a harmless and a crazy guy"

As they walked towards Henry's house James' anxiety rose, knowing that he might encounter something crazier than the previous time because of more people

"His house is extremely messy from inside and from outside too as you can see" "Don't react to it"

"It might cause some trouble for us"

"He will also try to change the topic from the prophecy; might even offer you some rum with milk, But you both stick to the topic and don't get entertained by his unnatural behaviour" said James as he warned Romilda and George about what they might witness inside.

The three of them, stepped onto the doorstep of Henry's house.

James gathered guts and knocked the door.

"Come inside" came a voice from inside

"Was that Henry??" asked George

"I believe that this is his house so he might be the one saying this" said James as he pushed the door gently inwards.

The voice of the door startled Romilda and George.

"What happened??" asked James

"The noise the door is making is creeping me out a bit" said Romilda

"Ok, there is much more to be creeped out inside" "Control your reactions"

They stepped in and found Henry in on his chair. The house was still messy with dirty clothes lying on the house, food fallen on the floor and dust running like a stream on the surface of every single metallic object in his house.

"Who is it??" asked Henry

"It is me Henry, I came here the other day"

"Oh yes, yes" "You will be James, right" said Henry identifying James

James gave a slight nod.

"I see you brought some friends of yours along with you" "I figured that you might come again but did not assume with your friends" "Never mind, I always keep a good stock of rum and milk"

"You all will be taken care of"

On hearing this, Romilda and George were frightened that they might have to taste the dreadful combination of rum and milk.

"No! No! we don't need rum and milk" "Will save that up for some occasion later in the week" said James

"Then what brought you here??" asked Henry

"Before discuss about that, this is George and this is Romilda"

"Ohh, pleasure meeting you people"

"I came here to complete our incomplete talk from last time" said James

"No! we did not have an incomplete conversation" "You got what you wanted from me" said Henry hesitantly

"Yes sir, for sure you did answer my questions clearly but I needed some more DEPTH and detail in them" said James

"Why did you need your fellow mates for that to come here though??" asked Henry

"I wanted them to come here so that they can get some of their queries of their to get answered by you"

"Ohh, I think that before a discussion, we might like to loosen up, don't you think the same George?" "Do you want some food??" asked Henry

"No sir, we are fine" said George "We just had our breakfast"

"Ohh, might invite all of you to my home for a dinner someday" "You would fall in love with the bacon and eggs that I make"

"Sure sir but… " said Romilda

"Oh, why not give you the recipe of my special dish so that you might be able to make it on your own at your place" "I might just go in and get the recipe written on a piece of paper "Just wait for a moment here and I will be right back with the recipe of the delicacy made by me" said Henry as he rushed into hi room.

"He is indeed acting weird" whispered George

"He is proving to be too good at what he does James" said Romilda

"What does he do good??" asked James "Changing the topic my friend" whispered Romilda

"He cuts us off before we even start conversing about the prophecy" said George

"He knows that but this is important for us and might just bring it out right now; I am not leaving from here without some information about the prophecy" whispered James

"Sure, try your luck mate but I reckon that we might leave from here soon empty handed"

"Keep some hopes at least George"

They waited for a while waiting for Henry to come out of his room but he was taking too long.

"He is taking an eternity for just writing the recipe" said George

"I think we should call him once" added in Romilda

Before Romilda and George could even think James called out Henry in a somewhat high pitched and loud sound.

"Henry, it is taking a bit too long" said James

"Yes, I am sorry to keep you waiting but the recipe is a bit special and lengthy so is taking some time to write it down" replied Henry

"It is fine Henry, we don't require it" said James

"No, I am already done with like half of the recipe, will be in your hands in some time"

"But I just recalled that we three are allergic to eggs and bacon; it makes us nauseous and causes extreme irritation so no point giving the recipe to us" said James trying to pull Henry out of the room by giving him an excuse

"That is peculiar but you three are from Earth so might digest that"

Henry started walking outside towards them and suddenly stopped.

"What about Andrew, he loves bacon and eggs; just take it with you" said Henry as he walked back in his room

"This man is driving me crazy, can't hold up with him anymore" whispered George as his frustration grew with time

"Control George, if we manage to get some information out of this person, it will help us a whole lot" "Keep your cool and wait for the result cause we are not leaving from here until we get what we came for" said James.

"I will try" replied George

Meanwhile they were cracking a long conversation about Henry, Henry was busy writing the recipe for the bacon and eggs inside the room.

Suddenly James walked into the room where he could see him sitting on a table with a piece of parchment and pen. The room was no better than the hall. James noticed an empty piece of paper with no trace of ink on it in

Henry's hand. Henry tried to hide it using his hand but his efforts went in vain.

"What happened James, why did you enter the room??" asked Henry in a monotonous tone

"Nothing, just thought of having a look at your room while you were diligently writing the recipe for the delectable meal for Andrew"

"Ohh, sure, you might consider having a seat" said Henry in a tensed tone.

"I am fine, had a lot of sitting to do recently" replied James

"As you wish"

"Is this the paper you will be writing the beautiful recipe on??" inquired James

"Yes, Yes, you got it right"

"Ohh, I caught a quick glance by mistake and saw that nothing was actually written on the parchment" "Is there anything wrong??" asked James

Romilda and George also walked in seeing James having a conversation with Henry.

"No, No nothing is wrong; it was just that I tore apart the recipe that I had written and threw it away on hearing that you three were allergic to bacon and eggs" replied Henry

"Ohh, where is the paper that you threw away then??" asked James

"Why do you need that piece of waste"

"I just want to see something; just answer my question Henry" "You are hesitating too much, is there something you want to tell us??"

"No, no, I don't have anything to tell you!!" "And about the previous paper, it might be in the dustbin"

"Do you keep a dustbin for a dustbin??" asked James

"What are you talking about??" asked Henry

"I am telling that you don't require a separate dustbin because I am standing in one right now"

On hearing this, Romilda and George were awestruck. The expression on their face changed and they tried to conceal it.

Henry looked at James with an intense look and stood up immediately.

"Why did you get startled sir, I was just kidding" "You know,there should be some fun elements in a serious situation to lighten the atmosphere" said James smiled cheekily

"Ahh, there is always some place for jokes in my place" "After all there cannot be eggs without its yoke" said Henry

"Sure sir" said James gave Henry a fake smile portraying that his joke was funny.

Henry grabbed a seat and by the time the tension in the room was settled, Romilda and George had come back.

"Any progress??" whispered George into James' ear

"No, just trying to shake him up a bit" replied James

"Do whatever you want to do, but we have limited time; it has been a while since we have been out" "In some time Andrew and David might be home waiting for us" whispered Romilda

"You guys are not helping me at all" "You were meant to pressurise him but you are putting pressure on me instead"

"What shall we do about it??" "He doesn't want to have a conversation with us"

"Ok, will do something about that but say something at least" "Don't stand here like living dead bodies"

"Ok, go ahead" said Romilda

"Hey Henry" "Meanwhile you are writing the recipe, let's have a conversation" "We are getting a bit too bored at this point"

"Yes, I agree with James totally" added in Romilda

"Ok, but I might not be able to answer everything as my focus is the recipe as you are so eager to have it" said Henry

"That can be kept waiting" said George "We are here for some days and don't need the recipe urgently" said George

"Yes, you can take the whole night today and give us the recipe tomorrow" added in James again trying to mock Henry

"Sure, Sure, but I don't think of delaying work"

"Ok, now let's talk about something else"

"Yes, what do we talk about??" asked George

"I remember that you had some questions about the prophecy regarding the prophecy Romilda" "That is the reason we came here; just got a bit distracted" said James

"Yes, you are right" replied Romilda

"Henry, do you know anything about the prophecy??" asked Romilda

"No, I only remember that it is an ancient object and might prove to be extremely difficult to find" replied Henry.

As he answered Romilda's question, swear dripped down Henry's shirt.

"You are sweating a lot Henry; you ok??" asked George

"I am good, I am good" "Sweating a bit because of the constant hand movement from the writing"

"You might consider taking a break" said James as he approached Henry's table and snatched the pen away from his hand

"What are you doing James!!" squeaked Henry

"You would not stop writing, that might cause some hand pain so I took the pen away" said James

"I am fine!! Give that thing to me back"

"Why are you getting so freaked out??" "It is just a pen" said James

"Whatever it is, it is mine and this is my house" "Give that to me right now" said Henry out of anger

Before James could make him anymore weird, he handed the pen back over to Henry.

"I am sorry but I don't like when people take my things like that and I can take care of myself" said Henry justifying himself

"Ok sir, I did not know that you don't like when we touch your stuff"

"I forgive you this time but the next time you did this, something might happen to you"

After saying this Henry went to the kitchen to get some water.

"Hey!! This man is crazy" squeaked George

"Yes James, I think that we should not stay here anymore or else this lunatic might do something to us" said Romilda

"And it has already been some hours since we have been here trying to get him to speak but this guys will not crack"

"Ok, Ok, we will leave right now but come back later again" said James

"Yes we will" "Now come on out, we must go as soon as possible"

They walked out where they found Henry chugging a glass full of whitish-golden liquid.

"Henry, we will take your leave now; Andrew and David might have reached back at home and must be waiting for us"

"You better do!!!" screamed Henry which startled all three of them

James observed the liquid he was consuming closely and discovered that it was rum and milk.

"He is drinking rum and milk; he offered me the same thing the other day" said James

"Let's go James!!!"

They ran out of the house as soon as they can.

"That man is mad, believe it or not" said Romilda as they walked down the road

"Yes, he indeed is a lunatic" added in George

The sun was already high up in the sky.

They had spent some couple hours in Henry's house. They rushed back to Andrew's house.

When they walked in, they searched for Andrew and David everywhere making sure that they had not come back till now.

"They are not home till now" said George

"Yes, I have searched everywhere" added in Romilda

"That is good for us" "By the way, I was thinking of telling Andrew about whatever happened today" said James

"But why??" asked George

"Andrew is the head of the council right now, he will be having much better ways to tackle this Henry guy" said James

"Before that lets take a final try and go back tomorrow; I overheard David today morning that they will be gone for some hours tomorrow too" said Romilda

"If we have some luck tomorrow, then we might be able to get him to crack open" said Romilda

"Sounds like a plan" said George "What do you say??" asked Romilda

"Ok, but this will be the last time we go alone"

On saying this they settled their conversation and rested for some time.

In some time they could hear the lift descend knowing that David and Andrew had come back

They walked back out finding both of them, hanging their bags onto the rack.

"How was your day at the council??" asked George

"Decent enough, can say that could have been more efficient and a fruitful council" replied Andrew

"Any progress in our case??" asked James

"Today, we had the council meeting regarding the village and not about you people" "The council members needed something regarding the village to discuss too" said Andrew

"Ohh, that is cool"

"Lunch is ready if you want to have it already" said Romilda

"Why not, have you had your lunch?" asked David

"No, not so early"

"Sometimes having it early helps" "Did not feel hungry until now and we decided to wait for you"

"It is fine, we will just freshen up and come back"

"Sure go ahead"

The day passed normally with no more activity. All of them rested on their beds or roamed around out in the market for some time to freshen up. Soon the ended with restlessness.

The next morning came up more beautiful.

Before either of the three of them could get out of bed, there came a noise early in the morning.

They opened their eyes slightly, gradually coming back to life from the lifeless sleep.

"Sorry to disturb you; just wanted to tell you that David and I are leaving right now" "We will be back by the evening" said Andrew

"Got it Andrew!!" said George

"Please do switch the lights off before leaving the room" said Romilda who was still in a deep sleep

"Sure" replied Andrew as went back out of the room proceeding towards another day of work.

James, Romilda and George went back to sleep and didn't wake up for some more hours

The sunrays slid into their room as Romilda opened up her eyes.

"Come on people; big day" said Romilda waking up George and James

"Yes, coming" said George as he gradually sat up on his bed.

James still lay on his bed like a lifeless soul.

"You better wake up James, or else I might have to use some methods to do so"

"Ok!! Waking up" said James as he sat up on the bed.

"You may leave the room now and get ready so that we both get a moment of peace" said George

Romilda left the room and waited for Romilda and James near the dining area for breakfast.

The morning was fresh and the pungent smell of the tea spread throughout the room.

"Tea is ready" said Romilda

"And so are we"

The three of them munched on their breakfast while talking about yesterday.

"Do you want to go today??" asked George

"Yes, we decided to" said James

"Of course we will be going to Henry's; we might be annoyed a lot by him but he does have something that we value" added on Romilda

"Ok, we are going today but you know the deal right; after today we tell Andrew about everything"

"Of course, we will do that"

The three of them got ready and left for Henry's house.

In some time they were in the midst of a busy market place.

As they walked past the bunch of people, they could spot the increasing amount of people entering the place.

In some time they surpassed the busy market place and approached near the castle. The castle gates were closed for some reason and a board was pitched outside of the garden of flower saying "Important council in work".

"What does this board mean??" asked George

"Don't know but leave it for now" said Romilda

In some time they approached Henry's house. As they stepped closer to the house, their anxiety levelled up contemplating about the actions of Henry they would have to face today to get some information out of him.

"He should be cracking today" said George

"Yes, after all, we are visiting him for the past two days" said James

"Not us, it is only you" added in Romilda

"Yes, if you put it that way"

In some time they found themselves on the doorsteps of Henry's house.

James gathered courage and rang the bell and waited for an answer from inside.

They waited outside for some time to get the usual call by Henry to come in but this time it did not come.

"Why isn't he responding??" asked George

"He might have not heard the bell; ring it again James" said Romilda

James rang the bell, not once but twice this time running out of patience.

There was no answer still.

"Let's go, he might have gone somewhere outside" said Romilda

"Let me try opening the door; he kept it open for the last two days" said James

"Go ahead"

James pushed the door but the door did not seem to move.

James pushed as hard as he could but eventually found it to be locked.

"He has locked the door" said James

"See, I am sure that he is outside" "No point staying here for any longer" "Let's go back"

Meanwhile Romilda was busy convincing them to go back, James examined the door closely.

"What are you looking at??" asked George noticing him gazing at the door

"I reckon that Henry has not gone outside" "He might be inside and known of the fact that we would have come so he might have locked the door from the inside" said James

"How do you know that he is sitting inside??" asked Romilda

"Look at the door, there is neither a keyhole or a latch or a keylock to lock it from the outside" "This only can mean one thing, he doesn't want us to even enter his house now" said James

"Yes, so either way, we cannot meet him now" "Let's go back"

"Stop Romilda!!" squeaked James

"We can have a look in the house at least".

James pulled Romilda back before she could walk any further.

"What are you doing!!" screamed Romilda

"Be soft Romilda, Henry will be able to listen us easily if you scream so loud" said George

"I am sorry, but James just pulled me back and my neck hurts now"

"Why would not I pull you back, you were just walking away before even listening to what I wanted to say"

"Ok, go ahead and complete your sentence now without any physical contact"

"Thank you, I just wanted to say that we can get a look inside from the outside" said James

"How will we be able to see inside??" "We don't have eyes which can look inside of objects"

"I am aware of that but Henry is a clumsy and a forgetful person" "You might have figured that on your own by now"

"Yes, he is but how does that help us??" asked George

"We can have a quick look for any open windows or curtains which are not drawn and look inside from there"

"I am sure he might have left at least some of them open, judging on how big of a lethargic person he can be" said James

"We can do that, but will it be right on our side to invade someone else's privacy in this way, taking advantage of the person's flaws??" asked Romilda

"Don't tell me that you haven't done something foolish or something wrong ever in your life!"

"I have of course"

"Ok, might as well do something else too" "After all, we don't intend to steal anything from him or harming him in any way"

"Ok, Ok, don't speak any further, start walking around the house" "I am tired of listening to you, it will be easy for me to do what you say" said Romilda in a frustrated tone

They started walking around the house, looking for any open windows or even a small space through which they could squeeze a look through.

Several twigs and pieces of branches lay on the floor causing some noise on their part. They had to be cautious on taking every step further aware of the fact that Henry could hear their movement from the inside.

"I don't think that Henry is that big of a fool" said George

"What do you mean??" asked James

"I mean he hasn't forgotten to close any windows and had drawn the curtains perfectly.

We can't even see a hole anywhere through which we can look inside.

After rounding around the house for twice they gave up.

"James stop, we have looked twice around the house now, there are no signs of what we are looking for"

"Let's go now" said Romilda

"I agree with Romilda mate, no point staying here now" said George

"Wait, let me think of something" said James

"There is nothing we can possibly do about our situation now" "Give up man" said Romilda

"Give me some time to think at least " squeaked James

As Romilda continued to convince James to head back, James kept thought of something.

"I have an idea" said James

"What??" asked George

"Wait a moment" said James as he headed towards the back of the house.

He picked up a branch fallen on the ground which was unusually long with a sleek end.

"What are you doing??" asked Romilda

"I am trying to get the window to Henry's fantasies open" said James cheerfully as he proceeded to a nearby window

"Ok, before doing what I want to do, is this the window to Henry's room??" asked George

"Probably not, as when we came here the last time, his room was somewhere in the front part of the house"

"Thanks George"

"Anytime" replied back George

Before both of them knew about anything the next thing that happened was that James had pinned the long branch into the mid-section of the window where the sleek end of the branch stuck between the two parts of the window.

"James!! What are you doing, get that thing out of the window" "We might be in a deep-deep trouble because of what you have just done" said George

"Wait and watch" said James as he throbbed the window as continuously in the mid-section where the mid-section existed.

In some time the window started to fall apart and soon enough they found the window panes fallen on the ground as two separate singular pieces.

Romilda and George gave out a slight shriek as the glass of the window panes shattered into a zillion miniscule piece. Meanwhile James was busy, drawing the curtains apart, Romilda and George stared at him in, stupefied by his actions.

"Have you lost your mind James!!" whispered George trying not to be heard

"Why are you whispering now, James has already made a ton of noise; there is no chance that we have still not been heard by Henry" said Romilda out of fear

"Hey, you both, stop talking, I am trying to do something here" said James as he opened the curtains.

Romilda grabbed him by the collar and pulled him back. James stumbled over Romilda's leg and soon fell on his back on the ground, with small pieces of glass shattered and scattered all over it.

"Ouch!!"

"What are you doing Romilda!!" screamed James

"What the hell do you think that you are doing" "Don't act foolish now and run with us" said Romilda

"Wait a moment" said James

"Look inside, I have opened the curtains and I think that we should go inside right now"

"Are you crazy!!"

"No, I am not" "Henry will not be able to hear us as this house is huge and won't be able to hear us from that room or hall" "Wherever it is where he sits" said James

"No! I refuse to take this risk" "You always convince both of us to do something stupid and in the end the three of us are in a deep trouble"

As soon as Romilda pelted all her anger out on James, she walked past George and James back towards their home.

"Where are you going??" asked James

"I can go wherever I want to" replied Romilda

"Romilda, stop, please!" screamed James

Romilda came to a sudden stop and in some time James ran towards her.

"Hey, I know what I am doing" "Just trust me and this time we won't get into any trouble" said James

"I am sorry but I have something in my mind" said James

"What is in your mind?" asked Romilda "Please enlighten us with your knowledge"

"I will tell you in some time" "Just get into the window with me for now and be absolutely quiet" said James

"This is the last time I am doing this James" said Romilda

"Ok, I won't ask you to do anything after today" "Just come in now"

They all walked in the backyard of the house where the broken window lay.

James climbed through the hole in the wall created by him. George and Romilda and followed him too.

They landed into a damp and dusty room now, with no furniture at all. All there was in the room was some paintings pinned to the wall.

The room was empty but in the far corner, ironically there was a broom which was cleaner than the surface of the floor.

The room gave out a pungent smell of dead mouse and rotten vegetables.

"Ughh! Who maintains this room" cried out George

"I don't know about you both but I am getting a sheer dejavu" said Romilda

"Seems like this is the type of room which led us into this world" said James

"You got it right"

"This is somewhat similar to the restricted room in our school"

"No, this is a lot different; that room actually had furniture" said George

"Forget the furniture, this is dusty and that was dusty too"

"Yes, nothing else matches" said Romilda in a low tone

"Lets proceed now if you are done talking about the previous room" said James

"But there is nowhere to go" added on George

"We are in Henry's house now and without his knowledge; we will have to look for something about the prophecy"

"There should be something in here related to that" said James

"There should be but I am sure that there is nothing in here which will help us" said George

"You sure that Henry will not come here James" said Romilda worryingly

"I am sure about that" "He is oblivious to the events happening around him and this room is significantly far from his room"

"He is a preoccupied nut head; he won't hear us at all."

"I seriously doubt you but am forced to trust you"

James gave a disappointed look towards Romilda showing his dejection towards her.

"That hurt a bit" he said gloomily

"Oh come on! Stop with the drama and continue with the work"

James continued to investigate the room but could not find anything in there.

In a matter of seconds he approached the door that would lead them outside of that dusty and dark place.

He gave it a slight push as it made a slight creek on every inch it moved.

"Why does every single door in this house make such a creepy sound??"

"Does he live in a museum or something"

"I don't know and don't care too" replied James

They walked out of the door and it revealed a corridor leading to the hall which they could identify the looks of it.

Suddenly they could hear footsteps in some distance and saw a shadow approaching near the corridor.

George was struck by panic and soon he started pushing away James and Romilda moving back into the room.

"What are you doing George" whispered James

Before George could answer the sound of the footsteps grew louder and in a matter of some seconds, James and Romilda had joined George into the room where they came from desperately trying to keep away from Henry.

"You could have told us before pushing us apart" said James out of anger|

"I could have but I could not think about anything other than how irritated I got when Henry was in front of me"

"I panicked and here I am, standing in front of you" said George

"Ok, shut up" said Romilda

James could hear some footsteps outside the door and covered Romilda and George's mouth in order to prevent them to blurt out any word from their mouths.

As the terrifying sound of them faded away he removed his hands from their mouths.

Instantaneously they began to cough and went on to cough for quite a lot of seconds.

"What happened to you both all of a sudden?" inquired James

"You put your nasty and shabby hands on our mouths" "You realise that when someone is talking, their mouth is OPEN!!" "You just put an awkwardly large amount of dust into our mouths" said Romilda as she stopped to cough

"Wait, my hands were clean" said James in confusion

"Yes, they were but you had a good idea of grasping a branch and breaking this window to get in"

"The branch would have been filthy as no one cares about cleaning a fallen and lifeless branch" replied George

"Ohh, I get it; I am sorry guys but someone just walked by in front of our door so I had to make sure, you did not speak anything"

"We can hear James" said Romilda mocking James

"We can talk about this later also" said James instantly trying to change the topic

"Let's go outside now." "I think we are in the clear now"

"Peek outside of the door once to confirm that" said Romilda

James bent down and slightly opened the door to allow enough space for his eye to look through the corridor.

"We are clear" said James

"But where will we go after we go outside??" asked George

"I don't know but we need to get pretty much the whole house and then we will be good" said James

"Wow, that sounds so easy" "Investigating houses with their owners living in them is a piece of cake for us" said George mocking James

"I am not kidding George, I am going, join me if you want to" said James in reply to George's comment

James pulled the door and squeezed his body out in the corridor. George and Romilda followed him but did not want to.

They tip toed their way to the hall where they found nothing but mess.

"There is nothing in the hall for sure" said George

"We came here the last time and he won't keep anything related to the prophecy here as this is a self-revealing place in the house"

"I agree with George; I reckon we will have to go with the rooms" whispered Romilda

Before they could do anything, there came a call from a distance.

"Thomas, you there???"

They recognized it immediately as Henry's voice.

In a matter of seconds they found themselves behind a couch.

"We are in a mess right now" whispered Romilda

"Shut up!" squeaked James.

"Thomas, you there!!" called out Henry as he walked into the hall.

He glanced at the place and did walk away after looking at it holding a transparent, glass cup in his hand which contained a goldish-white liquid.

James stuck out his head to look at what Henry was up to.

Henry turned into his direction. James panicked and soon he slid back behind the sofa entirely.

"I guess, I might have to have a nap alone today" sighed Henry as he walked into his bedroom shutting the door from outside.

"Has he gone??" asked Romilda

"Yes, he has gone" replied James

"We are good to go now"

"Who was he talking about though??" asked George

"God knows who"

"He said that he might have to have a nap alone today" "Does that mean that he sleeps with this guy named Thomas" said Romilda

"No! what are you talking about" "He is crazy but he is a man after all" said James

"It might be his wife or something" added on George

"Anyways he keeps a lot of secrets from all of the people in the village"

"Thomas sounds like a boyish name to me" said James

"Why do you care about Thomas so much James"

"We can talk about that later; let's do what we came here for first" said Romilda

"This girl got her priorities right" said George as he gave a slight laugh

"That was not funny George; you are right Romilda" "Let's go into the room by Henry's room but be absolutely quiet"

They approached the room right by Henry's room.

They gave the door a slight push to make sure it was open. The door opened with a jerk and slid past through the wall and ended up getting slammed onto the wall.

"What in the world are you doing James!!" exclaimed George

Before they could get caught, they went into the room, closing the door as slowly as James could.

"Why would you slam the door??" asked George

"I did not slam it; it just slid past right by the floor with the slightest amount of force applied on it" said James

"I am agitated because of this" "I reckon Henry might be coming after us any moment now" said Romilda in a low tone.

Before someone else could speak anything they could hear a moan from somewhere nearby.

As they turned backwards, they found a person lying on the bed with a thick blanket on him.

"Who is this now??" asked Romilda

"I don't know; this is peculiar" said George

"Stop talking and hide before he wakes up" whispered James

The three of them slid behind a stack of bags of grain. They ran downwards and lay there for some time.

The person did not seem to wake up but sometime later they could hear the door slam against the wall again.

It was Henry again.

"Ouch! This door needs to be fixed as soon as it can; my ears hurt like anything" screamed Henry

He closed the door gently and walked deep in the room.

"Ahh, here you are Thomas" said Henry

Meanwhile Henry walked near the bed on which the person lay asleep, James peeked at him through the gaps between the bags of grain.

"Why are you sleeping here??" asked Henry as he shook and woke up Thomas

"I was wearied out at work today; fell asleep as soon as I fell on the bed"

"You should have fallen asleep by me; it would have been a lot of fun" said Henry in an exciting tone.

"You are so naughty" moaned Thomas as he let his hand slide over to Henry's neck

"This is so peculiar" whispered George

Before George could speak anything else James shut him.

"Listen and be soundless" whispered James

As they gazed at the intimidating scene in front of them, they were left in awe.

In some seconds or so Thomas mumbled some words as he pulled Henry towards him as they started to passionately indulge into a kiss.

"What the hell am I watching" whispered Romilda

James again put his index on his lips indicating Romilda to be quiet.

As they watched the perplexed and disturbingly mad scene in front of them, they felt a feeling of discomfort passing through them.

Several seconds later Thomas' and Henry's lips departed relieving the awkwardness of the room which delved into the trio's veins.

"That was good" said Henry

"More like much more than satisfying on some other levels; it literally broke the passion scale" added in Thomas

"Let's go to my room" "We can have a nap together there" said Henry

"This room possesses a somewhat jarring look to itself if you know what I mean"

"Of course, I know what you mean, I actually feel what you mean" added in Thomas

On saying this the romantic duo departed out of the door slamming the door.

James, Romilda and George came out of their confinement.

"My eyes just bid my body farewell" said Romilda grasping her head form both her hands and tightening their grip to relief some tension gathered up in her veins.

"That was something unusual, I must say" said James gasping for breath.

"Come on now guys, that is nothing to be freaked about so much" said George in a monotonous tone

"What, you don't find that freaky??" asked Romilda

"No I don't because it is natural and we must act cool about it" "Nothing that was never known to us" said George

"Ok, I do think that we are overreacting a bit too much" said James

"Yes, forget about it and do what we came for" said George

"Right what to do next??" asked Romilda

"This room needs to be investigated" said James as he looked through the room once glancing at all the objects that the room beheld in itself.

"This room does not have anything to conceal" said Romilda

"It is not even well furnished like the other rooms that Henry has in his house"

"How many rooms have you been in till now Romilda??" asked George

"This is the third one"

"So you get it, right" said George. Romilda gave a slight disappointed nod, portraying the grief in getting proven wrong by George in a matter of seconds.

James opened up every drawer in the cupboard and found nothing other than dust and a magnifying glass in one of them.

"Why is Henry's place so weird" asked James

"Some people are just born weird" replied Romilda in a monotonous tone

"Ok, there is nothing in here" "Nothing under the bed, in the drawers or in the walls" "There is a bunch of garbage in this room" said James

"Let's go upstairs" said George

"There might be no other room on the ground floor"

"Where did you see stairs??" asked James

"When we were running through the corridor I saw stairs near the fireplace"

"You should have told us about this before"

"It just came into my mind right now" "So do we go or not??" asked George

"Of course we do"

The three of them proceeded outside of the room tip toing their way to the stairs. As they climbed the stairs, they found hundreds of antiques carefully arranged on the side walls of the stairs.

"Something feels creepy hear" "The house upstairs, is much better and cleaner" said Romilda

They approached the top of the stairs and walked into another corridor. It pretty much looked the same as the one which was below with wooden floor and the same amount of space with some rooms on the side.

"I think that we should go in this room" said George pointing towards the door right near the stairs.

"No, we must go somewhere, which shows signs of having any clues" "Henry's house is like a public guest house, full of rooms" said Romilda

"You are right Romilda but how do we figure out in which one do we go??" asked James in a low tone

"Just walk by the corridor and look peek into every single one once" "If the space looks suspicious, go inside"

"Sounds like something that we were already doing"

Soon they started opening and closing doors to multiple rooms and found a whole lot of décor in each one of them.

After some couple of minutes of touring them, they reached towards the end of the corridor.

James approached the last door of the never lasting corridor and found a plate pinned onto the door.

The writings were unclear because of a lot of dust which had frozen onto the plate.

James ran hands over the plate forcing the dust out of the plate.

Soon he could see the word "LIBRARY" engraved onto the plate.

"Hey, here is the last room" "This has a name plate on it which says library on it" said James

"Go ahead and open the door" "Anyways this is the last one which we need to go into" said Romilda

James opened the door and as he walked into the room his head entangled into a series of thin strings which seemed like a spider's web.

He removed it and saw nothing as the room was covered in sheer darkness.

"Move away from the door, let some light come in" said James

away Romilda and George moved allowing the light to surpass into the room.

The rays of light reflected into their eyes, through a mirror which was circular and had arti-craft of dragon surrounding the rims around it.

As they escaped the light and opened their eyes, they could see a majestic library lined up in front of them with numerous amounts of bookshelves in front of them.

"Looks like an old library" said James

"Interesting at the same time too" added in Romilda

"Want to look through this place??" asked George

"After all this is a library; what would it have except for books"

"This is the last place we can go through; why not just have a glance"

"Ok, I don't mind but after this we are going home because we will go back home"

"Yes, of course, what is there to even do after this" said Romilda

The three of them spread through the place looking for different sections and investigating single bookshelf individually.

The darkness that filled into the room did not help while looking into a thing.

James ran his hands through the bookshelves, removing some of the books to look behind them but eventually only found wooden back of the bookshelf.

In some time they had looked into every single section of the bookshelf and found nothing related to a prophecy.

"Is Henry a nerd or something" said James

"Might be, who else does have a colossal library like this at their home; I mean Andrew does not have one" replied Romilda

"Sure, this person might really be interested in history; I can see sections of only history of Meraki"

"I wonder, whether he would even have had some time to even read this" said James

"No, he might be busy hanging out with Thomas" said Romilda in a low tone

"Stop with that Romilda, I already told you about that"

As they talked, the door suddenly moved and gave a creek, arousing their senses.

"In some time they could see a shadow approaching into the room and before they knew anything else, they crouched to hide behind the bookshelf.

Henry entered the room along with Thomas and strolled around for a moment.

As they approached James, Romilda and George, they crouched and moved somewhere else.

The nearer Henry got to them, the more anxiety accumulated in their hearts.

They faced a roller coaster of emotions as they tip toed past Henry and Thomas' bookshelves.

In some time Henry and Thomas, both sat down with a book in their hand which they pulled out from a bookshelf far away from the door.

On the other hand, James, Romilda and George were on the other side of the library waiting eagerly for the two of them to leave the room as soon as they can.

They spent several minutes waiting in the corner.

"What do we do now??" "I can't sit here all day" whispered George

"I guess we will have to" replied James

"Why are you standing James??" asked Romilda

"To keep an eye on the door so that we know when they leave the room"

"Sit down, we can easily hear the noisy door from there" said Romilda

"Ok, that will do to" said James as he sat down on the ground.

As he leaned on the wall, a part of wall just rotated making him go into the hole in the wall.

"Ahh!!" came a scream as he went down the hole

"What just happened!!" squeaked George

Before Romilda could say something they heard Henry saying something.

"Did you hear that??" asked Henry

"Yes, it was like someone's scream" said Thomas

"Let's go and check"

Henry and Thomas got up and started walking towards the other side of the library.

"They are coming towards us" whispered Romilda

"Yes, I can hear them"

"I think we only have one option" said George as he looked towards the wall segment through which James went in.

"No, No, I am not going in" said Romilda out of terror

"You don't have an option"

On saying this, George grabbed Romilda by the collar and propelled Romilda into the tunnel.

After doing so, he joined her and slid gently into the segment making sure that he doesn't make any noise

He descended down a deep hole. George covered his mouth and grasped it tightly ensuring he doesn't make any sound.

He went deep into the tunnel for several seconds until the slide started to ascend. For a second or two, he was going upwards and was showered into the air eventually.

He fell on a bunch of hay wires and found Romilda standing right beside him.

"Where are we?" asked George

"We are somewhere known as a no-man's land" replied Romilda

"Where is James though??"

"He might be fine, pondering somewhere around here; now get up you or else I will pull you up"

"Ok, ok, wait for me to at least process what happened with us right now" said George in a frightened voice

They landed in a whole chamber. A pathway led to a giant structure and beside the path lay gallons of dark water laying lifeless and looking venomous at the same time.

"Where is James??" asked George

"Hi mate" said James as he came out from behind the hay.

"Hi James"

"Let's do this later and tell me this; why would you push me into this place??" asked Romilda

"Henry and Thomas were coming towards us and we would anyways have to come after James to rescue him. I could not do anything other than that" said George

"But how will we get out from here??" asked Romilda out of vexation

"I guess, we will have to figure that out with a calm mind Romilda" "There is no point pelting your anger towards us"

"We are trapped in the same situation as you are" said James

"I know but there is no possible way we can climb up that freaking tunnel and out of Henry's house"

"There must be another way to get out of this chamber" "We will have to figure our way out" added in James

"Let's go this way" said James as he started walking along the path towards the giant structure

"Why is this place so scary??" asked George

"Because this is beneath Henry's house I guess"

Drops of dark water dropped from the sealing increasing the anxiety and anticipation that had gathered in their heads.

The giant structure looked quite old as they moved closer towards it. Algae had spread like a virus all over the entire structure which was sculpted extremely carefully.

As they proceeded towards the gigantic structure; they looked for some gates that they could go through to get out of the place.

"There are no gates or further pathways that we can go through to get out of this place," said Romilda

"Yes, I figured that out" said James

"Don't you guys feel something weird about this place??" asked James

"Yes, of course" "It is beneath someone's house and there is no possible way to get out of here"

"No, this is beneath Henry's house, the person who holds the most amount of valuable information in the whole village" said James in a serious tone.

"This does mean one thing only that this place does have something to do with Henry and he must be knowing something about how to get out of here"

"After all, there was a clear pathway from his house to here"

"And who could have laid hay from beneath, the tunnel"

"This is all a setup for sure and the only person who can help us out of here is Henry" said James

"That is right" "That is a lot of contemplating in some seconds James but how do we get Henry down here??" asked Romilda

"He should be coming down here; given that he might have heard my scream"

"Why would he want to put himself into any kind of hazard and your explanation still remains haphazard James"

"It might be that he might be assigned this house and he might be unknown of the fact that a chamber like this might be existing down here"

"That does not make sense Romilda and I do think that we should focus more on getting out of here rather than just lingering about the topic 'What is this chamber about'" said George

"I think there is no option for us other than shouting out as loud as we can so that Henry can hear us" said Romilda

"That will surely not work but given that we don't have anything else to do, we can try doing that"

"Help!!" shouted out Romilda.

She continued to shout a couple more times but there was no response

"What are you both doing??" asked Romilda

"Watching you act like a hooligan"

"Come help me; don't watch"

"Guess, my throat will be sore in some time" "Had a cold drink last night"

They all moved towards the mouth of the tunnel through which they came into the chamber.

In some time they all were shouting out as loud as they can in hope of a response.

"There is no point doing this" "Let's go back towards the structure" "We might be able to get something near there if we search well enough" said James

They started back towards the structure.

Due to the somewhat narrow pathway, James was left on the sheer edge of the path. Due to the moist marble floor, he slipped and fell into the water.

"James!!" shouted out George out of shock.

"James come out of the water, you might sink" said Romilda

"Do you need a hand mate??" asked George

"Don't worry guys, the water is shallow and there is nothing in here to be scared about" said James as he got up.

"I am all wet now" "That was the best possible thing that could have happened to me"

James picked himself up. As he buried his hands into the water to touch the surface and get support to get up, he could feel a slight elevation on the right hand compared to the left hand.

He ran his hand through it and found it to be an object.

He clasped it tight in his claw.

Pulling it out he found it to be a box.

"What is this??" asked George

"I don't know, I just grasped it when my hand went into the water" replied James

"We can discuss about that later, get out of the water first" "You might catch a cold" said Romilda out of concern

James got up and left the pool of dark water handing the box to George. He started to vigorously shake himself to get some of the water out of his clothes and ears.

"What is this??" asked George

"Might be Henry's case or something" "Let's open it and check what is on the inside" said George

"It is locked; it has a keyhole" said George

"There is no key to open this thing up"

"This might give us some clue to get out of this place" "Honestly, I am not complaining but this chamber stinks"

"For sure this might be the oldest infrastructure in the whole of Meraki" said Romilda

"Romilda, you are not helping us find the key to this thing; help us"

"Look around; there must be something around here or else there is no way that we even have a chance of getting out of here" said James out of frustration

In a matter of seconds, the three of them, spread through the dark and dull chamber to look for a key.

Romilda, looked something near the hay they landed on. George went on and tried to figure something out near the pathway. Meanwhile, James tried hopping back into the shallow pool of dark water to try his luck for the key nearby too.

"Any progress guys?" called out James

"Nah" replied George with a disappointed grudge in his voice

"I can't find a thing and now my hair is covered in hay too" said Romilda

"Did you find anything from the little swim you had from in the pool??" asked Romilda

"Nah, seems like someone might have hidden the key somewhere else"

"Ok, Now I am not staying in this pool,and I might think that I would like to get out of this dark water pond" said James as he paddled his way out of the shallow pool

"Let me see the box again; where is it??" asked James

"Romilda has it"

"Hand it over to me Romilda"

"Yes, get it" said Romilda as she threw the box across the room.

James grasped it firmly in one hand and looked thoroughly through it.

Turning the box again and again, he searched for traces of key written on it

"There is nothing on this thing that could help us either"

"I reckon we figured that thing would be of no use" said Romilda

"You give up extremely easily Romilda"

"Stop it guys" said George disrupting the conversation

James continued to examine the box. He noticed a slight part of the box coming off. He tried pulling it out but it would not come out.

"Hey George, can you come here really quick??" asked James

"Sure, what happened??" inquired George

"Some part of the box seems to come out; it does not peel off" "Can you help me there??"

"Sure" said George as he grasped the box and tried pulling the portion of the box out" said George

"It is somewhat stiff, does not seem to come off"

"Yes, it is like stuck"

"Wait, I have an idea" said George as he proceeded towards the dark water and drowned the box into it. He vigorously rubbed it. Soon he let it out of the water and used all his power to get it out.

Soon, a part of it started to come off, revealing some letters written inside of it

"Good job mate" said James as George pulled out the entire skin of the box revealing a series of sentences engraved behind the box which were covered by the skin of the box.

"Romilda, I think that we found something; you might consider coming around here"

"What is it??" asked Romilda

"The skin of the box just peeled off and now we are left off with the backside with some engraved sentences on it" replied James

"Then go ahead and read them"

"Yes, I will do that now" said James as he began reciting the words that were written on the backside of the box.

James started reciting along the lines of the box. It said: -

*Let the faith of the old hail on you,*
*As they stand in front of you,*
*proud and loud, stands with a smile,*
*holding the key to your endeavours,*
*high above the ground,*
*speaks a million words without a sound*

"This is it, it ends here" said James

"But what does it mean??" asked Romilda

"Something that stands in front us and is a proud and loud??" "I am confused"

"I don't have any clue about what this person who has written this thing is trying to tell us" Sighed George

"Wait a moment, there is something in front of us" "Which should help us" said James

"But there is only a pathway and a bunch of dark water in front of us" "It is not, proud and loud" said Romilda

"I think that this is referring to the structure" "It makes sense because it is high the face has a smile on it" said James

"Yes, that is it!!" said Romilda

They dashed towards the sculpture.

"Does it say anything about where the key is exactly on the structure James??" asked Romilda

"No, it does not say anything like that" replied James as he came across the colossal sculpture looking for signs of a key.

James examined the rusty and the worn-out surface of the extremely detailed sculpture.

"There is nothing on the surface" "Let's look around the sculpture," said James

The three of them started looking around the structure.

They looked for something on the ground, scampered across end to end to look for the key but they had no luck finding the key.

"It should be in the structure for sure" said James

"But there is nothing on this thing" said George

"Search carefully"

'Believe me, you don't want to be trapped in here forever"

"What do you think I am doing??" asked George

"James, what if the key is in the structure instead of on the surface" said Romilda

"I do not think that they might be hiding it on the surface" "Try looking for some holes into the structure, any kind of compartment or any direction to the key" said James

"On it captain" said George

"No time to joke Romilda as around George" said she walked in slow from one side of the colossal to the other side of it in a distraught way owing to fear, anxiety, or other emotion:

trying to locate the key.

"There is nothing around here" said Romilda

"Look for the details" said James as he brushed past the structure.

In some moments, George and Romilda lay side by side dead on the floor while James tried searching for the key.

"The box thing is for sure to throw us off, I do not find any kind of key here James"

"I agree with Romilda; no point wasting our time doing something which will not result into something said George

"Is there anything else for us to do other than to get out of this place" "I reckon, instead of giving up, we should chase down on every single clue so that we at least have some chances of getting out this chamber," said James

"I do not think that there might be something that you might want from there" came a voice from a distance voice

The three of them looked into the far distance, only to gradually start seeing a person walking towards them, tossing a box in his right hand, while his left hand lay in his pocket.

Romilda and George stood out of fear and in a matter of seconds stood by James.

"Who is it??" called out James

"I reckon you know who I am" said the person as he came into the picture as the light reflected from his body into their eyes.

Soon they could see Henry walking towards them, still grasping the box in his right hand.

"Henry!! What are you doing out here??" inquired Romilda

"I might consider asking the same question to you!" squeaked Henry

"We, we just came by" said Romilda in a stuttering noise.

"I do think that you decided to break open a window and go through my whole house, ending up here in the end," said Henry

"That is somewhat right and might be wrong too" said George trying to contemplate Henry's thoughts.

"What were you thinking??"

"Ok, Henry, we know that you know that you know a lot about the prophecy, why else would you be doing such weird stuff in your house" said James

"No that is not the entire truth" "You believe it or not but that is the truth"

"Ok, I know about the prophecy but not entirely" "And I did not keep this information from you to not let you get back to your home or anything, neither am I selfish"

"Then why would you keep that away from us??" asked George

"I know a bit about the prophecy and the only thing I know about it is that it is somewhere around here in this chamber"

"But getting to it is the hardest and the most hazardous thing you can go through"

"I did not either of you dead by the time you reached back" "So I thought that I would keep contemplating the meetings of the council and of course you to keep you all away from the danger"

"Nothing else was my intent" said Henry

"It better be"

"Yes, I agree with Andrew" came another voice from a distance

"Oh, I forgot to tell you that I brought you a more of a reliable company" said Henry as the mysterious person approached near them, finally revealing his face to be Andrew

"Andrew!!" said George as leapt into Andrew trying to hug him.

"Ok, kid chill" squeaked Andrew out of pain

George loosened his grip onto Andrew

"Great, so what do we do next??" asked Romilda

"Like we do not have any other option other than to find the prophecy and get you to your world back"

"But we can also back to Meraki" said Romilda

"How, the place where we came from was another entry to this room, just from another room" "You can't get back up the tunnel to escape this tunnel" said Andrew

"So does this mean that you both are going to come with us to our world" said Romilda

"That is exciting, we can play PlayStation there at my place" said George in a low tone

"No! No, once we get to the prophecy, there is a way for us to get back up" said Henry

"Ohh, fine so now, we only have the task to find it"

"And that let alone is the hardest thing you have done possibly in your whole life and might even do ahead"

"I might have something to ease up the task"

"What??" inquired Romilda

Henry pulled out a small box from his coat pocket.

"What is that??" asked George

"I believe that you have managed to find the box in this dark water pool" said Henry

"Yes, we did, but we do not have the key to open it up"

"Well here it is" said Henry handing over the box to James

James opened the box up to get a carefully carved out lustrous key, made from gold

"Wait but the message on this box said that it was somewhere near the structure" said James in a shocking tone

"It was until my grandfather gave it to me" said Henry

"Wait, what??"

"You have the key, do not ask any further questions"

"Open up the freaking box"

"On it"

James grasped the key and shoved it down the keyhole and turning it around. The latch opened up and they pulled out nothing but another note.

"Another note I guess" said James

"Read it James" said Andrew

James went on: -

*Believe in what you don't*

*Trust the unthinkable and you find your way*

*The height is matched in the depth,*

*And the brightest of your endeavours shall be fulfilled by the darkest of the object*

*The direction maybe showed by ditties the eyes*

"I did not get it at all" said George

"It is rather short but so complicated at the same time" said James in a disappointed tone

"Think about something that is not usual"

"That is what we are trying to do right now"

"The height is matched in the depth, and brightest of endeavours must be fulfilled by the darkest of the object"

"We need to look for something that is dark and somewhat deep"

"Doesn't seem like there is something like that anywhere around here"

They kept pondering over the riddle until most of them gave up.

"I do not reckon that something around here correlates to that"

"Now THIS is the riddle that is trying to throw us off" said Romilda

"No, no" "The height is matched in the death, and the brightest endeavours lie in the darkest of the objects"

"It is the dark water!!" said Andrew

"It is dark and it can be deep in some part which we just need to explore"

"That is right!!" "But the there are several compartments of in which it is present" "Which one do we pick to go into??" asked Romilda

"The direction maybe showed by thc deity's eyes" whispered James in a low tone

"What??" asked George

"The direction maybe showed in the deity's eyes" "The eyes of the sculpture!!" "It has to be pointing towards one of them" said James

All of them looked into the sculpture's eyes only to find that it lay down on the right part side of the pathway and lay its vision on the first compartment in the queue.

"It is pointing towards the first one in the right-side queue" said Henry

"Yes, dive into it"

"Who will??" asked Romilda

"I guess, given that James is already quite wet from the dive he took before, he should be the one to go in" said George

"Yes, I am already drenched, I will go in" said James as he proceeded towards the first compartment.

He dived into the water. The water was much deeper than the other compartments. Water splashed out and made their legs wet.

James went into the dark water but he could not see nothing given the water was purely black in colour.

"I cannot see a thing" shouted out James

"Of course, you won't be able to" "The water is black in colour" "Try walking over the entire surface and as soon as you feel something off, inform us" said Andrew

"Got it" said James as he brushed his legs against the surface of the pool.

He wandered around for something until he got interrupter by something suddenly.

"Ouch!" screamed James

"What happened??" asked Romilda

"I just got stubbed in the toe!!"

"It might be the thing that the note was talking about"

"Yes, try burying your hand deep in the water and try pulling whatever it is out" said Henry

James reached down the pool and felt a latch on his hand. "Found it" said James as he pulled out the handle towards him.

The handle did not seem to come off due to the amount of water present in the pool.

James gave a jerk, applying a lot of pressure at the same time onto the handle. Soon the handle clicked in and the door that it was attached to just came right off.

Soon there was a whirlpool in the pool as the water drained down the doorway. James was also pulled downwards into the hole.

"James are you fine??" screamed out Andrew as he saw James getting into the hole.

In some time, James had gone down the hole with the water.

The rest of them rushed towards the whole and found a ladder descending down the chamber where James lay on the ground panting and catching his breath.

They descended down through the ladder and found nothing but a box several metres from them.

"James are you good??" asked Romilda

"Yes, I am fine, do not worry about me"

"What is that box??" asked George

"Not another box!!" said Romilda

"What do you think that is??" asked Henry as he helped James back up on his foot.

"I do think it might be another clue to the prophecy or the prophecy itself in it" said Andrew

"Then what are we waiting for, let's just go and get the box" said George as he walked towards the box.

As he took a step ahead, James pulled him back. An arrow ran past George barely touching him.

"This is why we should think before we do anything, you could have been dead in a second," said James

"Thanks mate" gasped George "Yes, you are totally right about that" "Getting to the prophecy is not a piece of cake" said Andrew "Good reflexes on your part James"

"Now how do we get through this??"

"I guess, I have a plan for that too." Said James

"What??" inquired Andrew

"We can use the box and throw it on the tiles to trigger the tiles" said James

"No that would not be enough pressure for them to even trigger" said Andrew

"Do you have any long thing that we could use to do so??" inquired James

"No I guess, I do not have one"

"I do have one" said Henry as he pulled out a short pipe out of his bag. "That will not do Henry, it is too short" said George

"You have to wait and watch" said Henry as he flicked his hand and the pipe was into a long stick.

"Now that will work"

Henry handed over the stick to James. James went on and put the stick on the tile in front of him. He applied gentle pressure onto the next tile and found another arrow passing right by him.

"Careful James" said Andrew as he tried to caution him of the incoming arrows.

One after the other, the arrows came by as James dodged each one of them.

In some time, they had reached the box.

"Finally!!' Sid George as he grasped the box and picked it up to find a shiny prophecy inside of it.

"Wooahhh!!" said George admiring the prophecy.

"We found the prophecy!!" screamed Romilda

"Wait, let me examine it first "said Henry as he picked up the prophecy onto him. He examined the surface of the prophecy and found indentations and several scratches on its surface.

"Someone was right in saying, all that glitter is not gold" said Henry

"What do you mean??" asked James

"This Is not the real prophecy, it is a fake one" replied Henry

"How do you know that??" asked Romilda

"The real prophecy cannot have any action of indenting or the state of being indented.

or any scratches on its lustrous and majestic surface"

"This is a fake one"

"So what do we do now??" asked Romilda

"I guess, we cannot do anything else other than to wait" said George

"No, we can't just wait here forever"

"I think we should break the prophecy like the previous one" "The previous one sucked us in when it was broken" "It is a risk but clearly there is nothing else we can do about it," said Romilda

"That is right, we can do that and have to do it at this point" added in James

"I guess there is only one option then" said Andrew as he caught hold of the fake prophecy and smashed it down to the floor

The prophecy shattered into millions of pieces.

"At least tell us that you are breaking it before doing it" said Romilda after giving a slight shriek.

In some time, they could feel several vibrations in the ground. Soon the walls turned around and they found several small and big weapons smeared onto the walls. In front of them, came down a dark coloured man with a wand in his hands. His face looked wicked and he carried an evil smile on his face. He was covered in a black coat and had two swords and a shield in hanging onto his back.

"Who in the world are you??" asked George

"I am."

"Helda" said Henry before the person could complete with his sentence.

"Yes that is right and I guess you know a thing about me"

"Maybe more than what you think" said Henry with a hint of fear in his voice

"Wait, how do you know this person??" asked Romilda

"I have heard of this warrior in the books about the prophecy, he protects the prophecy" "We are extremely close to the prophecy" whispered Henry

"Yes, you are but nowhere close to it" said Helda

"What do you mean??" asked James

"You have proved your wit and courage by coming till here but now you need to portray your strength to truly earn the true time travelling power of the prophecy" said Helda

"What do you want from us??"

"I thirst for blood, your blood, and you shall for mine" "From now on, you all have to fight me" "You defeat me, you get the prophecy" "You are not able to, you are dead" said Helda in a low tone.

"DEAD!!" squeaked George

"Yes, death shall approach your fate, no backing out now" "The room shall be locked and it may turn into an arena"

"No, No !!" screamed out Henry

"You know that you are the strongest to fight the battle for the prophecy" "This is unfair" said Henry

"If you cannot defeat me, you do not earn the prophecy over me"

"I guess we do not have any other option other than to fight him" said James

"Grab a weapon" said Helda as he threw several swords in front of their legs.

All of them picked one and grasped it tight in their hands. Their anxiety and fear came out in the form of fear as several emotions were pelted into their heart by Helda.

"In some time you shall witness, what you call the bloodshed" said Helda as all the possible routes for escaping the chamber were closed and they were left alone with the deadly warrior.

He pulled out a sword from out and started walking towards the 5 of them.

"Guys, do not be nervous" "Be courageous, if we win this fight, we get to get back to our homes" said James

Before anything else could happen, Andrew went on to give one blow to Helda. He was blocked by Helda and thrown away into the corner by him.

"Nothing to fear right James"

"No, I am not feared" said James as he proceeded in front of Helda

Helda swung his sword, but James nearly dodged him. James put a short into his torso but the thick sword was put in front of him. Andrew tried attacking him from behind the back but the shield blocked the fatal blow.

James was pushed back by him and a series of unordered attacks were directed towards Helda by Henry, Romilda and George who soon landed on the ground after that.

James, went on and kept attacking he was exhausted. "I do not think that there is any way to defeat this demon" said James to Andrew who sat right by him

"I guess you will have to pull out some options from your bag"

"I am on it, meanwhile you distract Helda from everyone" "I will figure out what will work on him but I will need some sort of distraction"

"I got you but I do not think that we have much time here so please do whatever you do extremely quick," said James

James went towards Helda and started trying to bash him with the swords again but only ended up failing all of his swings on his shield or his swords. Romilda lay lifelessly on the side exhausted from trying to fight Helda while George was bleeding in the knee. Several drops of blood covered the floor as the battle went on.

James kept dodging all of his blows to keep away from the menace that Helda could cause him.

In some time Andrew came in blasting a potion onto his head into his eyes.

"Now!! James, his vision has been blurred" screamed out Andrew

James swung his sword into his face making a cut near his left eye.

The creature screamed in pain but went on to rage even more.

He pelted darts into different directions. Everyone crouched down to escape the darts. In some seconds Andrew came onto Helda again, breaking a vile of a poisonous potion on his face again.

"These are stupid games you kids are playing with me!!" screamed Helda

"These stupid games will kill you and you will experience death in some seconds." Said James angering Helda furthermore.

Soon every one of them held a scar from the ferocious strikes that Helda struck him with. Everyone lay exhausted on the sides with Helda in the middle screaming to make them furthermore scared. "Please spare us!!" cried out Henry as he crawled onto Helda's feet. "Now you see my true power" screamed out Helda

"Yes, we do and we are sorry to disturb your slumber like this" cried Henry

"Do not beg in front of him henry!!" screamed out James from a far corner of the room

"I do not have any other option, I care about my life more than anything else in the entire world," said Henry

Helda began to laugh as his pride swallowed him.

Suddenly Henry grasped a vile of potion from under his coat and splashed it upon his face again. He grabbed his armour and ripped it apart to expose his chest and stomach.

Until then Helda had fully recovered and soon stubbed the sword through Henry's chest.

"No!!!!!" cried out Andrew as he saw Henry fall onto the ground. Andrew crawled near Henry, just beneath Helda trying to help him stay conscious.

Helda had already initiated another fatal kill towards Andrew and had held up his sword right up in the air. Suddenly, James stabbed him from behind in his torso multiple times making him fall to the ground.

"Is henry, ok??" asked James "He is breathing but we may soon lose him" moaned out Andrew

James pulled out the gigantic metallic sword from his chest.

"Don't you have any potion or something, I surely think that we can save him!!" said Romilda

"Pass me my bag George" said Andrew

He searched through his entire bag and pulled out a reddish-orange vile out of his bag. He opened it up and poured it all over the wound.

"This will only keep him alive for some minutes" said Andrew

"I think Andrew we will have to let him go" said George

"No!!" "That is my friend you are talking about George" "He is not going to die, not going to die" moaned Andrew in pain.

Meanwhile a doorway opened in the room. James frantically went in to find something that might help Henry.

He found several plants in there and in the far corner of the room, there lay a magical prophecy which shined bright, spreading its magical light in the room.

He walked near the prophecy and found a board in front of him directing towards the plants. The board said

"For healing the courageous"

James quickly ran out and called Andrew

"Andrew, I guess this might help Henry" Andrew followed James to the plants.

As he approached the plants, he quickly recognised them.

"These are the magical plants that heal every single wound" "These have been searched upon for years" said Andrew as he plucked the leaves of some of them.

He ran towards Henry mashing the leaves using his hands. He applied the paste onto his wound and found it stitching itself together.

Henry startled and woke up. "He is up!!!!" shouted George out of happiness.

"Yes he is" said Andrew as he hugged Henry twice.

Andrew helped him upon his feet.

"Thanks for saving me, Andrew!!" said Henry thanking Andrew

"It was all James" said Andrew

Henry extended his gratitude towards James. "Thanks a lot James"

"Any day Henry" replied James "By the way, I have found something that might interest you"

James led them to the prophecy.

"This is the prophecy, this is it!!" "This is the magical belonging of my ancestors!!" cried out Henry

"Yes, it is" chanted Romilda and George

"Now we can go back home" said James

There was a long silence in the room.

"I think it is time for us to part our ways Andrew" "I enjoyed my stay here in Meraki and thanks a lot for helping us through this journey" said Romilda

"My pleasure, thank you to help us find the long lost medical remedial treasure of Meraki James"

In some seconds, they fell into a tight hug and bursting into tears.

"Say goodbye to David on our behalf" said George

"I will" replied Andrew

Andrew grasped the prophecy and gave it to James.

"It is time for you three to go home" said Andrew "How will you both get up??" asked Romilda

"Do not worry about us" replied Henry

The three of them put their hands on the prophecy as they bid their final goodbyes to them.

In some time the prophecy sucked thcm in.

In a matter of seconds they found themselves on the floor.

James, Romilda and George were back in the room where they came from.

The three of them woke up and found themselves in school

The school bell rang and everyone was rushing for their next period by the sound of it.

"I guess, this is it," said James

"We are back home!!" squeaked George

"Yes, we are!!" said Romilda

The three of them held each other's hand and walked into the school hall corridor with expectation and aspirations.

They delved into the crowd and continued for their next lesson.